Flight of the Green Bird

a novel

"the web of our life is of a mingled yarn, good and ill together"
William Shakespeare

Myra S. Shapiro

authorHOUSE®

AuthorHouse™
1663 Liberty Drive
Bloomington, IN 47403
www.authorhouse.com
Phone: 1-800-839-8640

First published by AuthorHouse 7/28/2009

ISBN: 978-1-4490-0378-4 (e)
ISBN: 978-1-4490-0379-1 (sc)
ISBN: 978-1-4490-0381-4 (hc)

Library of Congress Control Number: 2009906712

Printed in the United States of America
Bloomington, Indiana

This book is printed on acid-free paper.

DEDICATION:

To my six wonderful grandchildren, Jenna, Alyssa, Ethan, Justin, Noah and Zoe, who fill my days with joy and laughter and life cycle events to live for; to my children, Marcy and Eric, and Bruce and Marcie, whose continual support and love fill my heart with sunshine and gratitude; to my husband Harry, whose patience and constancy make me whole; and to friends and soulmates who fill in all the rest of the spaces.

Special thanks to my valued friend, Barbara Roberts, whose incisive observations of an early draft of this book led to a much better outcome.

FLIGHT OF THE GREEN BIRD

Prologue

By the year 2024, the industrialized nations of the world had made major advances in energy innovation. Political turbulence, fluctuating oil prices, and hard-hitting global warming soothsayers, were the drivers of these sweeping advances, which took place in dramatic ways and with enormous speed.

A combination of stringent fuel regulations on new vehicles and mandatory fleet modifiers on existing ones, up-to-the-minute nuclear power plants, satellite driven solar panels and wind turbines, tidal energy conversion methods, multi-based bio-mass distribution networks, clean coal and synthetic liquid gas delivery systems, had significantly reduced the world's demand for oil. This decrease resulted in an 80% decline in market share for the oil-rich Persian Gulf region. Consolidated oil markets such as OPEC, a cartel that coordinated most of the world's oil product, were near collapse with barrelhead prices declining to their lowest recorded value. More alternative energy sources and a rival cartel's outer-continental-shelf oilrigs in North America, South America and Africa, were expected to come on line by 2030 to further reduce the market for OPEC oil.

Recognizing this reality, nearly all of the oil producing nations of the Middle East had joined the developed world to embrace technology innovation and build 21st century economies. As a result, they were wholly integrated into the world marketplace.

Hindered by self-deception, the rulers of Saudi Arabia and Iran, formerly the leading OPEC players simply turned a blind eye to the changing tides. Though the writing had been on the wall for almost three decades, these stubborn stragglers refused to face the new reality. With petro-dollars in scarce supply and already miserable living conditions deteriorating fast, they were urged by their angry subjects to reform or step down. Threatened by growing pressure, these theocrats, titled potentates and so-called elected leaders, mostly old men in gilded cages, were frantic for solutions.

In the spring of 2026, the Iranian President and the Saudi King, each accompanied by trusted advisers, met under their golden domes and forged a marriage of convenience. In mutual self-interest, these long time adversaries concocted a plot to break the top-secret energy security cyber-codes that kept the wheels of the industrialized world turning. With the unprecedented power that would come with these codes in their hands, they would disable the cyberspace engines that managed the energy infrastructure of the West and incite panic.

Armed with knowledge that ground based computer networks controlled both the electricity grid and the nuclear power plants, that equator satellites covered the earth's entire surface to operate solar grids and wind farms, that communication satellites synchronized tidal conversion equipment, ran clean coal transmission lines, managed bio-mass distribution centers and regulated the steady flow of synthetic liquid gas, they planned to crash these cyber-systems long enough to cause massive disruptions. They would bring the industrialized nations to their knees begging for Persian Gulf oil; beginning with the nation Iran considered their archrival for world supremacy, the United States of America.

To execute this plan, they would seek out vulnerable men with dirty little secrets to hide or greedy people more than willing to sell their souls for big money. They would find them, and they would destroy anyone who stood in their way. If this plan did not succeed, they would devise another. Nothing could stop them. They would not be deterred from their ultimate objective, the restoration of their fading power.

Like rolling stones gathering bittersweet moss along the way, the lives of those snared in this conspiratorial web would change forever. It is said that a spark of the divine is concealed in even the most evil acts. We shall see.

Chapter 1

The day began like most steamy summer days begin. In the pastoral setting of Laurelwood, the red-hot sun sat on the landscape as if an accomplished painter had thoughtfully placed it just behind the hilly knoll. Its early morning rays touched down on the broad green lawns that surrounded this country estate, swept along the wooded drive, grazed past the underbrush of rhododendron and mountain laurel and moved on to brush the corner of Senator Winston Ainsley's second floor bedroom balcony. The estate, marked by a familiar signpost along the winding rural road, lay nestled in the midst of a grassy valley of Potomac horse country, thirty minutes yet a thousand worlds away from the shrill noise and hectic pace of the nation's Capitol, a quiet sanctuary that gave Winn shelter from the maddening crowds.

As he did most summer mornings, the Senator stepped onto his balcony for his morning ritual. He was a striking figure, his mane of snow-white hair and piercing pale blue eyes set in a sun-bronzed face, his tall, athletic build impeccably dressed in a well-tailored Brooks Brothers suit, an immaculate white Hugo Boss shirt and his signature polka-dotted bow tie. He read his text messages, scanned the Web, and then glanced in the usual order through the three newspapers neatly placed on a round marble topped table. If he missed anything important he knew that on any typical morning, when he arrived promptly at 8 o'clock at his high-ceilinged walnut-paneled office in Suite 203 of the Old Senate Office Building, his alter ego, Griff Foster, legal counsel to Winn's Senate Intelligence Committee, would provide an executive summary of all the hot news he needed to know. The summary, double-spaced and never more than two pages long would be placed precisely in the center of an enormous antique table, a family heirloom that served as his desk. Winn knew this day would be different.

As usual, Charles, the faithful family houseman who had looked after him from the time he was a teenager and had come along to tend him after he married and moved into his wife's childhood home, brought Winn's breakfast to him. It was always the same – two cups of strong coffee in a Sheffield silver pot, a small pitcher of whole milk, two slices of buttered whole grain toast, two selections of marmalade and six-ounces of fresh-squeezed orange juice in a sparkling Waterford tumbler. Each item was placed on a well-polished silver gallery tray covered with a starched Irish linen placemat and napkin. Winn still longed for a cigarette and restlessly reached for one, forgetting for the moment that he had abandoned that habit years ago.

A lot of newsprint on the new intelligence estimate but no mention of a security breach, and on this morning he was grateful for that. The press conference was scheduled for 4 o'clock. That would give Griff the time he needed to set up his end, and then Winn could blow the lid. He steeled himself for the chaos that would surely follow.

With the methodical mind of a cautious man, he reviewed in his mind's eye the events of the past two days just to make sure they were not a figment of his imagination, a manifestation of a very bad dream. He relived with some satisfaction the pleasures he had enjoyed two nights ago, the same sensual pleasures he enjoyed every Tuesday night at the well-secreted white palace that existed mainly to satisfy the sexual desires and fantasies of the powerful men who controlled the nation's Capitol. It was just something he did for the past fifteen years, a standing appointment every Tuesday at seven to safely and anonymously take care of his carnal needs for the week. As always, his mind drifted to Celeste. He would have preferred to make love to her, but he could barely remember how it felt to hold her close, to inhale her fragrance and caress her well-cared-for body.

Fifteen years had passed but the memory of that last time still seared his brain when he thought of it. In the first aftermath of that terrible night, he agonized that she would never forgive him. So many years later with so many lost opportunities to bury the incident and move on, he worried that he could never forgive her. He suffered bouts of profound loneliness, painful times that came late at night after they had spent an enjoyable social evening together. In those dark hours he was often struck by a strong urge to escape the emptiness of his room, and he would wander onto his bedroom balcony to seek comfort in the stars. But these moods were stubborn, and he learned to wait it out, knowing that eventually the mood would pass. Still, he was grateful that he and Celeste maintained a careful, polite and even affectionate demeanor around others, and this cordial public face would have to do for now.

When they first met, Celeste was a popular debutante, once described on the society pages as "a beautiful brunette with the willowy figure of a cover girl and the graceful stride of a gazelle." Greatly admired in privileged Washington circles not only for her beauty, but also for her sharp mind and her Ambassador father's valuable political connections, she was courted by an endless procession of suitors. She chose Winn, and they were married within six months of their meeting. Now, when he reflected on their brief courtship, he wondered if her gently probing questions were more about the political partnership he could provide than about him. Yet there were times when he glimpsed real affection in those expressive eyes of hers, green catlike eyes that drew him to her from the very beginning.

They met at an exclusive party for the Maryland Hunt Cup steeplechase races, held annually in the valley of the aristocrats, Winn's home turf in up-country Baltimore County. The gathering was set up for a small group of favored and fashionable elites in a special enclosure separated from the casual observers who lined the wooden fences of the participating farms. Celeste and Winn knew a lot about this time-honored timber race, a risky sport across the rough terrain of field and stream with twenty-two formidable jumps, some up to five feet high, a grueling course where it was rare for an entire field of horses to finish. For reasons that neither of them could explain, they hadn't attended this big event before and their rookie enthusiasm for the local horseflesh and the amateur blue-blooded jockeys who dared to take up the challenge, kept the early conversation going.

The party was located at the difficult 13th jump, named the Union Memorial, after the Baltimore hospital where riders who fall and injure themselves were often taken. Their host, a friend of Winn's who knew them both and thought they would be ideal together, introduced them. Winn was running for public office, Celeste was comfortable in the public arena, and in the beginning, they were as their host suspected they would be, a perfect pair.

In some respects, Celeste was her father's daughter and like him, her political instincts were impeccable. Until now, Winn had made no important public move without running it by her. But this one was dicey, and he had carefully avoided any hint of it. He wanted to insulate her from any nasty repercussions, and he was sure that so far he had succeeded.

This past Tuesday night was like no other. On this night, the usually unseen Madam X sought him out. The Madam, an Asian with an exquisite round face and a tiny graceful figure, was wearing her customary outfit, a long pencil-slim dress of gold silk damask adorned only by an enormous pear shaped diamond fixed to a nearly invisible neck chain. On his way out, she asked that the Senator come to her office. With the easy familiarity that spoke of their once intimate relationship, she took his hand and led him down a dim back passageway and up a narrow staircase, motioned for him to enter the door that was directly at the head of the stairs, and she slid away.

The room was softly lit with wall lanterns hung at appropriate places on heavily textured grass cloth walls. It was expensively furnished in muted shades of cream and gold with an antique Chinese rug, a six-panel incised Asian floor screen, an elegant seating area and a small desk. A young man, who Winn had seen tinkering around the place, stood swiftly from the low-slung sofa and extended a clammy hand but did not introduce himself.

In a hushed voice, the man claimed he had stumbled upon stunning information while he was engaging in his nasty business, his nepharious pursuit of "black hat" computer hacking. He did not disclose that even in his tender years he had already earned a notorious reputation in the burgeoning underworld of computer hackers where he was called the "locksmith," the undeniable master of computer-intrusion tactics. He justifiably claimed that his decision to disclose the data he had unlocked put him in serious personal jeopardy, so immediately after this conversation he was returning to the soft bosom of a far-off hideaway, far, far away from trouble. As he told an astonishing story, the evidence of his nervousness came in rivulets of sweat that dripped from his oily pockmarked face and in big wet patches that spread from his armpits down the sides of his denim shirt. With permission, the Senator taped the conversation, and for the next 30 minutes he listened in disbelief and suddenly realized that he was barely breathing.

There are those awful life-changing moments; ugly drops of time when you know that nothing can ever be the same, when you wish you could turn back the clock and erase the horror. For Winn this was the moment, and he knew he had better play this hand carefully and with all the skill he could summon up. If the informant was on the mark, he had less than seventy-two hours to shut down the coup.

By Thursday morning, with expert planning and secrecy, Griff had laid the groundwork and Winn was ready. He glanced at his watch and saw that he had just enough time for a second cup of coffee before his driver came by for him. Then, abruptly emerging from the quiet blue sky, he heard the loud sound of a small plane or helicopter. In this posh neighborhood this was not a foreign sound but the engine noise sounded too loud and too low. Winn turned to scan the horizon and was shocked to see a helicopter swooping towards him. He stood swiftly to escape to the safety of his bedroom, but his last thoughts were that he wouldn't make it. It was up to Griff now.

At exactly eight minutes before seven o'clock on the morning of Thursday, August 13th, 2026, the praiseworthy public life of United States Senator Winston Ainsley, the scion and the last survivor of a long line of prominent and privileged Ainsleys, was done. The strafing from the helicopter sliced him almost in two, splintered the balcony doors, shattered the powdered brick and splattered blood everywhere. The remnants of his final breakfast lay on the fractured marble table and his future lay butchered on the marble floor.

The helicopter spun away, climbed above the hilly knoll and blew up in a fireball brighter than the risen sun. Finger on the trigger, wide grin on his face and fervent prayer on his lips, the triumphant pilot believed with every fiber of his being that he was about to enter the Gates of Paradise.

Chapter 2

Still groggy from only two hours of solid sleep, Griff rolled off Senator Ainsley's worn brown leather sofa and headed for the Senator's private washroom, which was conveniently tucked away just inside his office. He splashed cold water on his face and borrowed the Senator's electric razor to shave the prickly stubble that covered it. He had pulled many all-nighters in his twenty years on the Hill but the last two nights were the toughest he could remember. Since it was critical to keep his work under wraps, he had prepared the statement, the press handout, and the subpoenas in solitary confinement. As far as he knew, other than the conspirators and the disappeared informant, only he and the Senator knew the details, and they needed to keep it that way. Now, they were ready to push the buttons and disrupt the plan.

Griff's cell phone rang. At 7:05, Griff answered and the Senator's driver delivered the news. He was shocked but some corner of his brain told him that he had almost expected something terrible to happen. He stumbled onto the sofa, leaned his forehead into his cupped hands and thought hard. Then he got up, went to his computer, made a hard copy, wiped the hard drive clean, destroyed the backup copy, put the hard copy, the memory chip, the subpoenas and three handouts into a manila envelope and left for the staff parking lot where he had stashed his yellow Volkswagen beetle. He placed the envelop in his glove compartment and locked it, headed back to the office, half walking, half jogging, and primed himself to face the staff.

By 8 o'clock, most of the staff had arrived. They were huddled in clusters looking like frightened deer caught in the headlights. Some were sobbing, others stoical, teary-eyed or too dazed to speak. The phones were ringing and no one was answering them. No one was sitting at his or her desks. The computers were on but no one was paying any attention to them.

Griff knew that he had to get through this day with a semblance of calm. He had to bury his pain and close his mind to the heavy lump in his throat until he could think this through. Was he safer blending into the disorder or should he just hightail it out of there. He decided it was smarter to go underground, but he would make an effort to provide a cover story to pave the way. He put a new message on the answering machine and brought the staff into the Senator's office. Mitch, the administrative assistant was missing. Griff found him tucked away in his office with the door shut, working away at his computer as if this was a normal day, and Griff asked him to join the staff meeting.

Speaking to the assembled group, Griff directed Mitch to take charge, turn all press inquiries over to the FBI, contact the Governor's office for guidance on how he wanted them to handle inquiries related to succession, refer constituent inquiries to the junior senator's office and suspend other ordinary activity until further instructions. He didn't mention who would give the instructions because he didn't know. Mitch insisted that he wasn't up to the task, but Griff refused to take no for an answer.

With his heart pounding so hard that he thought everyone could hear it, Griff said, "Listen guys, I don't know what the hell happened but I've got to get out to the Senator's place. Mitch, I know this is hard, but you will just have to rise to the occasion and handle things here. It's important that all of you stay put until you've been interviewed." Not likely, but if any insiders were involved, he hoped he had bought some time. If they had tagged Winn, he could be next. Who had known that Winn was about to reveal a nightmare; that he was about to expose a secret network buried so deep in the bowels of the faceless bureaucracy that it could remain unmasked forever? Did they know that Griff had been in the loop all the way?

Griff could feel the sweat rolling off his neck but he also knew that if he succumbed to the fear that gripped him, if he took off in panicked flight, if he reached for that first drink, he could be a dead man. He told himself that he had to stay cool; that he was the only one left who could stop these people from wreaking the havoc they intended. He walked briskly to the parking lot and slid behind the wheel of his car. If only he hadn't chosen the flamboyant yellow bug that was so out of character for his conventional persona. It was a fleeting thought. He knew he had to ditch the car in any case.

For the past few months, his elderly parents had abandoned their Federal style Georgetown house for their contemporary villa in the south of France, taking cooking lessons of all things. In his memory his mother had never cooked, and his father didn't even know where the kitchen was, but he supposed this was as harmless an activity as any for these septuagenarians, and he smiled in spite of his state of fear. He headed for their garage, which housed only an aged Mercedes reserved for the unlikely chance that their driver failed to come by for them. He would stash his car there. At least it would be out of sight. He drove up Wisconsin to the alley behind P Street, got out, opened the heavy wooden doors and pulled into the space next to the Mercedes. Then he closed the garage doors, bolted them and exited through the garden door.

Griff took a deep breath and sat down on the white marble bench that was his mother's favorite garden spot, the place she labeled her "contemplation corner." God, he needed a drink, but he knew he couldn't let his anxious feelings lead him to the transient relief he once found in booze. He knew it would only lead to misery on the other side. He gripped the bench until his knuckles ached and tried to plan his next move.

He was clear headed enough to know he had to survive long enough to expose the conspiracy. The informant was gone. He couldn't bring in the Agencies because he didn't know if they could be trusted. He didn't know if there was anyone he could trust. He knew he would be tested, that this dangerous journey would make him vulnerable to his own private demons, but he had to stay focused. He had to stay alive.

Chapter 3

On Embassy Row, at the Iranian Embassy in the 2500 block of Belmont Road, Ahmed Tehrani, an incredibly handsome man in an elegant black silk shantung suit, double breasted with deep side slits, entered an ornately gilded lift and rode to the basement. He placed his hand on a door pad and the door opened.

A pious man, Ahmed took his well-worn Koran from the inside pocket of his jacket. Left to him by his martyred younger brother, he was never without this holy book of divine guidance, a book he had been taught to revere from his earliest memory. He read his favorite chapters, savored the sacred words, and he waited.

Just as he hoped it would, Thursday, precisely at 7 o'clock on the morning of August 13th, the phone rang. He opened the bottom drawer, picked up the secure cell he had hunted up on the black market and heard Hamid say the pleasing words that stilled his thumping heart, "Allah be praised, the job is done. On the other matter, we need three or four days! You should know, there is a loose end. Do not worry. I will handle it."

A grinning Ahmed returned the cell to its cradle, and kneeled on his prayer rug.

"Allah hu Akbar. Allah hu Akbar.

Ash-hadu an-la, Ila ha-illallah

God is great. God is great.

I bear witness that there is no God but God."

Satisfied that he had sufficiently humbled himself before Allah, he returned to the phone and pressed number 7. Abdullah al Omari, his Saudi counterpart, answered.

"My dear friend Abdullah, the job is done," said Ahmed. "I have spoken to Hamid. We are working on the finish line. Three or four days! You should know, there is a loose end. No need to worry. Allah be praised, Hamid will tie it."

"He must not fail," replied Abdullah.

Abdullah turned to his companions and said, "Ahmed and Hamid are not to be trusted. We are the true Muslims. They are infidels, and you must watch them. When we have finished this mission, we shall speak of this again. Peace be upon you."

"Allah hu Akbar."

"Allah hu Akbar."

Chapter 4

Celeste stirred but remained in a half sleep. In the dark realm of her nether world, she saw the engine of a train bearing down toward her, and she fled toward an escalator that vanished before she could reach it. It was always that way with her nightmares. She was running through a fog and her means of escape would move away and disappear. The noise of the engine became unbearable, moving closer and growing louder. She suddenly realized that she was not dreaming. She was awake and her worst nightmare was just beginning.

On Wednesday, August 12th, the day before Winn took his last breath on earth, Celeste attended high tea at the opulent Iranian Embassy. It was an invitation she coveted ever since they had re-opened, and she never missed the opportunity if she could help it. At the reception, the usual tea sandwiches and miniature scones were artistically arranged on engraved sterling silver trays set between enormous flower arrangements and Tiffany candelabrum. The tables, dressed in formal linens reminiscent of the old days of British influence, were positioned beneath a gleaming minaret shaped gold dome that rose from the ceiling and spread its sparkling flashes of gold light onto the silver below. Tea napkins with the embossed symbol of Iran were placed on the buffet and near the tea and coffee service. No alcohol was served.

The Embassy was furnished with antique Persian rugs, the kind that had once been made by the tiny fingers of indentured little children. The fine rugs were strategically placed on well-cared-for marble floors and hung on intricately designed blue and white mosaic walls. On some walls and ceilings, there was elaborate mirror work, crafted by mirror artists who lived at the Embassy in lifetime sinecures from the regime. These artists learned their craft from their fathers and grandfathers who had learned theirs from the generations before them. It was the kind of proper atmosphere that suited Celeste, and she dressed very carefully for it, wearing designer make-up that left no hint of imperfection and elegant clothing that bore no obvious trace of extravagance. This was her way of assuming the public role of the late Ambassador's daughter and the esteemed Senator's wife without having to tap into her own private persona and that suited her just fine.

As usual, Sally Burton was there. Sally, editor of the Style section of the long-lived and still flourishing Washington Post, was a regular guest at the soirees of this favored Embassy. She made sure that flattering descriptions of its social gatherings appeared in her column and that occasional features of its envoys were assigned to her most popular feature writers. In return, her frequent invitations to the Embassy gave her enough grist for the mill for at least two of the sometimes-cutting articles she wrote each week. She was definitely not mean by nature, but she tried to satisfy the cloying Embassy gadflies who often contributed useful little nasties to her column. With a little stroking, they would continue to feed her the gossip that enticed political junkies to read her articles before they read the front page. If that meant an occasional snide remark, she remembered to balance it with sugar in another column.

Sally noticed that Ahmed, the cultural attaché, was giving Celeste his rapt attention. She wondered if something was in the wind for these two, and she decided to keep an eye on them. It was rumored that Winston and Celeste lived in separate wings of their home, yet they seemed to share a genuine affection for one another. Sally sighed and thought to herself that the rich are different and did things their own way. Perhaps on a slow day, she would dig around and see what she could unearth.

Bored by the same old faces and the lack of scintillating repartee, Sally left the Embassy party early for her small townhouse near the Hill, an eye-catching pad for which she had paid an astronomical sum. She poured a tall vodka and tonic and sat out on her small but skillfully landscaped terrace garden. In her routine way she tapped out the report on her laptop while the details were still fresh in her mind. In the event she picked up more tidbits at Ainsley's press conference, she decided to hold off filing until Friday morning, sometime before the noon deadline

Thursday was not an unusual day for a press conference on the Hill but a press conference called by Intelligence Chairman Ainsley was almost unheard of. He rarely sought out the cameras. His reputation as a straight shooter on foreign affairs and a man of substance on security matters had served him well, and he managed his exposure with well-covered major speeches in academic venues and carefully chosen hard hitting Senate hearings, which he controlled. The Sunday talk show hosts also sought him out and made sure they threw the softballs that assured his return appearances.

To get some background on the press conference, Sally put in a call to Griff. The receptionist knew that Griff always took Sally's calls so she gave the call to his top aide.

"Griff is tied up, but I'll have him call you as soon as he's free."

"What's with tomorrow's press conference?" Sally asked. The aide replied, "Beats me. No one is talking. I'll probably find out the same time you do, but if I hear anything earlier, I'll buzz you."

Sally did not typically cover press conferences, but her curiosity was piqued, and since she could pretty much call her own shots, she decided to attend. Her gut told her that something was up and her gut was more often on the money than not.

Chapter 5

Griff's action plan was developing in his mind. He was going to disappear, stay safe until he could set up a way to explode the bombshell.

His parents, former Ambassador Arthur Foster and his wife Pamela, Washington Establishment figures famous for their influential political entertaining, usually squirreled away enough cash in their safe to take care of the help they engaged for their frequent dinner parties. Most were moonlighting from their jobs as headwaiters at the State Department or the Senate Dining Room or some other government venue and would work only for cash, a tax-free benefit they felt entitled to receive.

Griff knew using his laptop, his credit cards or his cell could track him, and he figured he needed some cash to support him for now. He opened the safe, which was concealed on the staircase wall behind a portrait of his paternal grandfather and found about $1400 carelessly tossed inside. Just in case he needed more, he took some bearer bonds and left a brief note in the safe. His parents weren't expected back for another month or so, but if they showed up he knew they would trust him.

With reddish hair, sapphire eyes and a lot of freckles, Griff worried that if they were looking for him he would be easy to spot. He couldn't do anything about the freckles, but his other traits were manageable. He found his old electric razor still sitting in the bathroom cabinet where he had left it. Much to his mother's wide-eyed chagrin, he had used it to carve his favorite football team's logo into his college brush cut. He plugged it in and shaved his head clean.

In his old room, which was exactly as it had been twenty years before, he changed into some old college jeans that were actually loose on his lean jogger's body and put on some worn loafers and a dingy "Beer Rocks" t-shirt. He found an old duffle on the closet floor, threw in a heavy hooded sweatshirt, some socks and underwear, the razor, an old toothbrush, and a couple of t-shirts. He took an unused cloth money belt from his chest drawer; one that his parents had given to him for his après college treks to Europe and India. It would come in handy now. He stashed the cash into it, shoved the bonds to the bottom of the duffel, sat on the edge of the bed and tried to pull himself together.

Griff had already taken on the look of a drifter. To beef up the look he was going to do something he had always wanted to do but never had the nerve to do, even when he was flying three sheets to the wind. In any case, he couldn't hang out here much longer. He retrieved the envelope from his glove compartment, put it in the zippered compartment inside his duffle and left through a passage beside the garage. He followed P to 29th and went down M Street a few blocks toward the river to the Jinx Proof Tattoo and Body Piercing shop, a curious place that he remembered from his early days of exploring beyond the loose boundaries his mostly absent and indulgent parents had set for him. He selected a popular serpent pattern, had it tattooed in black on his left bicep, had his left ear pierced in two places and bought small gold earrings for it, selected a neat pair of wire-framed amber tinted aviator shades, paid cash, and took off.

He would disappear for now, but he worried that no matter how far he ran, the dreaded pale horse would ride his shadow. He needed a drink, but he recited in his mind the mantra he learned at rehab, and he buried the urge.

Chapter 6

Akin to older brother and constant friend, Charles was bound to Winn as if by blood and was plainly devastated by his violent end. His loyalty to Winn had never wavered but, from the beginning, he was captivated by Celeste. He carefully hid his feelings because he knew they couldn't lead anywhere but now, with a loving heart, he would help her get through the anguish of this day.

Long ago Charles decided that the façade that Celeste presented to the world was just that, a façade, and that beneath the exterior coolness; there was a flame that ached to burn. Servants talked to one another, and he learned that Celeste's childhood had been difficult, that her overbearing father had done a real number on her as well as on her meek and submissive mother. They were both gone now, and he had never heard Celeste mention them.

Charles took only a moment to yield to his own grief, then consciously donned a stiff upper lip and walked swiftly up the back stairs to Celeste's suite. Her door was ajar and the housekeeper was with her. Charles looked in tentatively but Celeste rushed to him, put her head on his shoulder and began to sob.

"This can't be happening, Charles, he can't be gone, he can't be!" she cried, "We're so unfinished. I have to speak to him, to tell him why. Take me to him, Charles, please take me to him."

This would be difficult. Charles knew that Winn's mutilated body would be a memory too painful for Celeste to bear. He made some inquiries and was relieved to hear that the room could not be entered until the coroner and the police were done. He would see to it that Celeste saw Winn only after the funeral home made him more presentable.

For hours Celeste alternated between pitiful sobs and soft weeping, sometimes covering her red and swollen eyes with her hands as if she were trying to block out the present. After a while, Charles led her to the chaise and sat beside her. Celeste wept until there were no more wet tears left to fall. Extreme exhaustion crept into every bone of her body, childlike whimpers escaped her aching throat, and she curled up into a ball as if retreating into the womb. Charles tried to comfort her but she would not be comforted.

"Why did this happen, Charles? Why would anyone do such a horrible thing to this good man? Where is Winn? I need to talk to him. Why do I feel so empty, Charles? Please don't leave me, too."

"I'm here, Mrs. Ainsley. I'm not going anywhere. I'll be right here."

Chapter 7

Thursday, at 7:30 in the morning, both Sally's phone and alarm rang at the same time. Her boss, Washington Post publisher, Maury Feld, was on the line. Wow! The sky must have fallen. She saw him at the annual Holiday party, but that was it. Feld rarely communicated directly with the Style section, and Sally couldn't imagine why he was calling her.

Feld, which everyone called him including his wife, was an enigmatic figure in Washington political circles. No one knew where he stood politically, and he wanted it that way. What they didn't know was that he judged a man by the nature of his deeds and the strength of his character and didn't care a hoot about his party affiliation. He never sought to put his own personal stamp on the paper but depended on the diverse opinions of his well-regarded editorial board to produce cocktail party fodder for the intelligentsia. However, his editorial board members understood that Feld had keen intellect, was a lifelong student of just about everything and everybody, and that he would interfere only if they did sloppy work or tried to shove the truth under the rug.

A slightly balding and stocky man of medium stature and a pleasant enough face, Feld arrived in his office every weekday and Sundays at 7:30 AM, and left promptly at 6. As a rule, he didn't second guess his managing editor's decisions on the work of his reporters unless they failed to meet Feld's high standards of civility, balance, diligent fact checking and at least two solid sources. Although they might argue over whether these standards were met, on these matters they usually accepted that Feld had the last word. They also understood that if his anger was sufficiently aroused, he was very likely to explode and their familiarity with these infrequent but memorable events kept them on the straight and narrow. Occasionally, Feld had his editors send terse memos to all of their reporters, careful not to single out any one of them, to remind them that opinions belonged on the editorial page or in the blogs but not in their news reporting. Everyone knew the memos really came from Feld, and they usually knew why.

Feld, who had inherited great wealth from the entepreneurial endeavors of his two sets of immigrant great-great grandparents, was a religious man. Although his parents had turned their backs on Jewish practices, Feld returned to his roots and faithfully observed the Jewish Sabbath. His respectful staff knew better than to try to reach him on Friday night or Saturday, at least until the sun went down. He was a charitable man but very few knew this because he contributed to many of the causes he believed in as an anonymous donor. Only his devoted wife, Sarah, and his teenage daughter, Melanie, knew for sure that he was a softie, even a pushover for a good cause or for them, and they were careful not to take advantage of him. Feld's rabbi also caught glimpses of his true nature when Feld was given the honor of carrying the Torah or chanting to the Congregation from its ancient scrolls. What's more, the rabbi knew that the synagogue could depend on Feld to cover its annual deficit with enough money each year to keep the budget in the black. The rabbi would find a subtle way to mention the figure, and in a day or two, he would find a check on his desk for that precise amount.

Feld said, "Senator Ainsley was murdered less than 30 minutes ago. Turn on your TV while you dress and get over to Ainsley's house. They've probably got it roped off but get what you can. I know this isn't your beat, but you know the Ainsleys and you can add a human-interest twist until we can get the hard stuff. Sally, you and I will work together on this. Stay in touch through my office." His office? How odd!

Griff still hadn't returned her call. She had a queasy feeling in the pit of her stomach. She would try to reach him as soon as she got behind the wheel.

Making the careful choice of her "chic simplicity" look, she selected her caramel colored silk slacks with its matching long-sleeved shirt, her favorite bronze Gucci belt and her outrageously expensive Donald Pliner chunky heeled chocolate colored low boots. She tucked her videophone into one of the side pockets of her old brown leather Prada tote, slipped on her diamond-studded steel Fendi wristwatch, and glanced into the full-length mirror mounted behind her door. Assessing her appearance with a discerning eye, she decided to add gold disc earrings to frame her natural ash blonde shoulder-length tresses, brushed blush on her fair-skinned cheeks, and spread tinted gloss on her pretty lips. She threw her most reliable laptop into the tote, grabbed her Channel horn-hued oversized sunglasses from her foyer table and only twenty minutes after Feld's call, she was out the door.

Sally slid behind the wheel of her two-seater Porsche and pulled away. With hard-earned self-confidence, she knew she looked great. She felt ready to tackle the day no matter what it threw at her. Two irrationally suspicious and abusive ex-husbands and a few ill-fated relationships behind her, she was relieved now to make her own way. Her uncanny intuition told her this would be a good day for her already ascendant career, and she would try to make the most of it. She wondered why her intuition, which was so on target for most things, consistently failed her when it came to the men she brought into her life. She punched Griff's number on her cell, but no answer.

When Sally arrived, the narrow lane leading to the Senator's estate was already a jumble of cars, cameras, grumbling reporters and video trucks. Yellow tape was stretched along the road and sawhorse barriers closed off the entryway to the gates. Local police cars and state police vehicles protected the entrance and a covey of policemen tried to keep reporters behind the ropes they had erected along the lane. There was an occasional opening for vehicles, and Sally managed to locate a space that accommodated her car. She was glad she had worn the chunky heeled shoes. They helped her maneuver the swath of rutted grass that lined the roadway.

Sally sought out a familiar face among the police crew and located a former Capitol policeman who had landed a good job with the Maryland State Police. She sidled up to him, and in an engaging manner, reminded him of their friendly past encounters and gently tried to get any information he might have. She didn't press him because she wanted to be welcome to come back to him later, but he freely volunteered that the FBI, the CIA and the National Transportation Agency had been called in and that a press conference would be held as soon as a decision was made on which department would coordinate the players.

This was hard news, the kind that would keep the front office going until she could announce the time of the press conference. She contacted Feld's office. Amazingly to her, he personally took her call, and she brought him up-to-date. She also told him to be on the lookout for the feature she would file through his office in the next hour.

Sally had clawed her way up from Inquiring Reporter to the social pages and then to Society Editor. She thought she was a good editor, careful not to cross the legal boundaries even when she skirted the edge and never gave the managing editor a reason to call her down. She couldn't imagine what had happened to abruptly catapult her upstairs. Her gut told her there was sub-text to this, and she figured she would find out what it was before this story was done.

Making her way back to the car, Sally sat in the passenger's seat and tapped out the report on the Embassy gathering. She held all the drivel about the other guests for another day and focused on Celeste, adding more background about her and today's events. She read it through and was satisfied that it was good work. Keyed up by the karma of her moment, she was sure this story would earn a frontpage byline. It would be her first.

Her work done for now, the chaos of the day suspended for the moment, she allowed herself to think about the tragedy of Ainsley's murder. He was one of the good guys, and she truly regretted his end. She tried Griff again. Still, no answer!

Chapter 8

Press was descending to the site en masse – the electronic news hounds with their video phones, the international press, the Capitol news reps, the dailies sending in backup, the weekly magazines, the yellow rags, all lined up and trying to find a spot to park their cars, their video cameras, or just themselves. The police had closed off the lane on both ends. The lucky ones like Sally, who had arrived early enough, had their spots inside. The others had to scramble to get as close as they could or find a way in, but the State police were remarkably efficient at keeping them out.

The local police chief, Duke Connelly, a ruddy, gruff and affable bear of a guy, had risen through the ranks and felt more than a little intimidated by the presence of the academically schooled State police, most of whom had attended or taught at the John Jay College of Criminal Justice. Still, it was his territory, and he would make sure that they gave him the lead. He had been police chief for only fifteen months and this case could put him on the map.

Colonel James Devlin, Chief of the Maryland State Police for over twenty years, was a respected fixture on the Maryland political scene and seemed friendly enough in a courteous kind of a way. He didn't have to prove himself to anyone, and Duke hoped Devlin would give him a break.

There were Secret Service and FBI floating around, and by the high and mighty looks of them, Duke figured they were trouble. He decided he was going to make the first move to schedule a press conference or at least announce an anticipated time. He chatted with Devlin, and convinced him that it would be just a preliminary announcement to keep the swelling press crowd at bay. Strictly a traffic and crowd control problem, which was his job! They set the time for 4 o'clock.

Duke worked the crowd just to let everyone know he was there and stopped to chat with anyone who seemed interested in chatting. He would make his presence known, especially to the press. Sally, with an indefatigable news hound's nose for expanding her network, recognized the opportunity and took it. Duke never missed reading her column, and he was flattered that she spoke to him and tapped his name into her notebook. He had his people set up a lectern, made sure the connections were there for the microphones, checked the sound system, and had some folding chairs brought in and placed in rows in front of the rope line. He would reserve them for the speakers and a few select press members, and he would see to it that Sally had a front row seat.

For him, this was the big time; he was a big man today, and he was all pumped up. He phoned his wife and told her to be sure to watch the newscast at 4 o'clock. Then he walked up to the house, nodded to the Secret Service agents guarding the entry and went inside. He had no particular destination. He did it just to see if he could.

Chapter 9

A few days earlier, in the sub-basement of the State Department, in a mostly forgotten safe room near the Situation Room, three men huddled over brown bag lunches. All three looked as though they had been cloned in some laboratory specializing in State Department high-level but underpaid career personnel. Buttoned-up, tight-lipped, rhep tied, and dour, they spoke to each other in the same monotonous tone that made it difficult to distinguish one from the other.

In a mind-numbing way, they spoke of the bloodless coup that would swell their lean pockets, and they spoke of the offshore bank accounts that had been established for each of them. Then they opened the lunches made for them by their dutiful wives, retrieved bottles of water from the small refrigerator, and made college football small talk while they chowed down their respective tuna, egg salad, and ham and cheese sandwiches, all on bland white bread. They glanced at their respective Timex stainless steel watches and rose from their chairs.

"Are we clear on our assignments?"

"Perfectly clear."

They nodded in agreement. All three took the basement elevator to the lobby. Then, two of them walked to the bank of elevators that would take them to the Near Eastern Affairs floor where their respective Saudi and Iranian specialist desks were located, and the third took the private elevator that led to the floor for Assistant Secretaries.

At approximately the same time, two White House NSA staffers were meeting for lunch in the bustling cafeteria of the House Longworth building where the noisy crowd provided a high degree of anonymity.

One passed to the other a piece of paper with the name of an offshore bank account along with the account number.

"All set?"

"Affirmative."

They finished the navy bean soup, which was the specialty of the cafeteria, split the turkey sandwich that was the special of the day and returned to their respective desks, one in the basement of the West Wing, and the other one tucked away in the bowels of the Eisenhower Office Building.

The next day, in the left front corner red velvet banquette of the Russian Tea Room in New York City, two well-dressed men with steel grey hair and engraved silver cufflinks to match were lunching with an equally well-turned-out woman. They were sipping giant martinis while devouring a shared $400 first course of four ounces of beluga caviar, which they mounded on silver-dollar-size blinis. They followed this with tasty Russian borscht with sour cream and finished with sweet tea.

"Arrrangements air-tight?"

"They are."

The woman gave each of the men a slip of paper with the name of an offshore bank and an account number with instructions. She paid their bill and they left, two for their UN Mission office and the woman for her office in the suite of the Secretary-General.

In L'Enfant Plaza in the Capitol, two young men in khaki slacks and open-throated striped shirts sat on a bench in the center square. They wore similar NASA photo identification tags on long chains around their neck. They chatted and one gave the other a piece of paper with an account number and the name of an offshore bank neatly written on it.

"You okay with this?"

"Not really. Do I have a choice?"

"Guess not."

They sat for a while and then headed back to the NASA high-rise office building that dominated the Plaza. They entered the building, nodded to the long-time security guard, hopped on an elevator and got off on different floors, one floor with "Cryptography" etched into a glass entry door, and the other, "Secure Zone," with a keypad affixed to the door panel.

Chapter 10

Twenty years on the Hill, fifteen of them with the Senate Intelligence Committee, Griff considered his options. He had more than a few connections in the underground world of phony passports and false identity papers, but he didn't think he needed them for now. He had enough cash, but it wouldn't last forever. He needed to play it safe, get out of town and hole up someplace out of harm's way until he figured out what to do.

He walked and jogged a few miles to the Greyhound Bus Terminal behind Union Station. As far as he could tell, no one was following him. He picked up a bus schedule and shopped for someplace where he could easily be lost in the crowd. As luck would have it, in less than half an hour there was a rest-stop-only bus headed for Chicago. Griff decided to be on it. From a rusty vending machine, he bought a cup of black coffee and sat on a wood slatted bench in the rear of the dilapidated waiting room. The coffee was as bad as it gets, but he needed it. Two TVs were blasting, each on a different channel, CNN on one, and an old boxing match on the other.

A news alert was flashing on CNN and a newscaster repeated the earlier news that Senator Ainsley had been assassinated.

"The Senator was an exceptional asset to his country. He was one of the truly good men, a man who never shirked his heavy responsibilities as Chairman of the Senate Intelligence Committee, who pursued them with vigor and who carried them out with patience, fairness, and keen intellect. He served this nation with distinction and honor, and he will be sorely missed. Why he was assassinated remains a very troubling mystery. He had called a press conference, rare for him, and it was scheduled for 4 o'clock this afternoon."

"This just in – Sally Burton of the Washington Post has been at the scene since shortly after the Senator was murdered and has been providing helpful updates through the Washington Post blog. She reports that Montgomery County Police Chief Duke Connelly has announced a news conference for 4 o'clock, ironically the same time that the Senator had intended for his own. At that time he will be prepared to announce how the investigation will be coordinated and who the lead spokesman will be. Of course, we will carry the news conference, and we will stay on this story as new information comes in. The President is scheduled to speak to the nation any moment now. We hope that he will be able to assure us that this was an isolated incident and that the nation's leaders are not in imminent danger. This is the legitimate concern we all have at this moment, and we have been assured that every precaution has been taken to keep them safe."

Sally! They were steady dinner partners, and he relaxed on her patio almost every Friday night with a root beer and a coterie of her close friends. He knew that she counted him among them, and he was pleased that she did. Sally had been through some nasty relationship disasters just as he had, and they often commiserated with each other, using the sharp barbs and black humor that served to dull the hurt. They were on the same plane intellectually and were never bored when they were together. Their friendship remained platonic because neither wanted to chance losing it. He needed an ally, someone he trusted, someone who could expose the security threat in one large dose to a wide audience. No telling if this conspiracy was more widespread than he knew and that was one way to get it out safely. Sally fit the profile, and aside from that convenient fact, he really wanted to talk to her.

In the meantime, he told himself that the President was a very savvy guy who was undoubtedly doing everything within his considerable power to get to the bottom of Winn's assassination. Griff hoped the wheels had begun to move without him.

The bus to Chicago took off at noon with Griff in a rear seat. He looked around at his fellow passengers, and he was satisfied that he seemed to blend in. There was a long ride ahead, probably 14 hours or more when he would own the luxury of anonymity. It would give him some time to surrender to the grief that kept welling up in waves in his gullet and to think about his next move.

Chapter 11

Celeste's doctor arrived and found her agitated and disoriented. He administered a shot and convinced her to sit up and take some pills. She held on to Charles' hand with a fierce grip and wouldn't let go even when he gently tried to dislodge it. After a time, Celeste's grip relaxed, her body uncurled, and mercifully, she passed out.

Somewhat dazed when she awakened, she found her room filled with grim people. Who were these people, she wondered. They looked like Secret Service, men in dark grey suits, old-school-ties and earplugs and wires dangling from their ears and a woman in a pants suit that mimicked the same look. Calmer now, better able to cope, she realized that she was in a dressing gown, her hair was mussed and she had no makeup on. She needed privacy. The doctor was still there, and her housekeeper, and a confusing mix of strangers. She realized that privacy was a luxury she was not likely to get.

The lead Secret Service agent introduced himself and explained to Celeste that he was there to assure her safety and help her over the next few days in any way he could. "Where is Winn? I want to see Winn! Please!" With no family left to console her, no siblings, no children, no parents, and few real friends, she had little choice but to depend on the kindness of strangers. She had political friends of course but their friendship was fleeting. In the "beltway bubble," where power is the coin of the realm, where favors are cynically banked for exchange, she no longer had anything of value to offer. Maybe they would hang around until the writing was on the wall, until they knew if she would remain in the loop, even succeed Winn. They would surely stay close until after the funeral, which was sure to be loaded with dignitaries.

Celeste was regaining her bearings. She wanted to be sure that Winn had a proper send-off. Where was Griff? He would know what to do. He knew all of Winn's friends, all of his political alliances. He would know how Winn would want to handle this. She asked the agent to find Griff and bring him to her.

Instead, Mitch showed up and explained that Griff couldn't be located. Celeste thought to herself that maybe he had headed for the nearest bar and was somewhere drowning his sorrow. She didn't blame him.

Over the next few days, the agent was indispensable to Celeste, and Mitch hung around doing little things. There was a lot to do, so many decisions to make, the official ones, the ceremonial ones, the personal ones. Strangers would help her with all of them but then, Celeste thought they would disappear without a backward glance.

The President spoke to Celeste, and offered to send Dee, his Chief of Protocol, to assist her for as long as she was needed. Dee arranged for Winn's flag-draped casket to be placed at the Rotunda of the Capitol for public viewing, for the funeral service to be held at the National Cathedral and for his burial at Arlington National Cemetery. Always, Charles was there to tend to her personal needs and his presence was a comfort.

Dee made sure that Celeste was consulted at every turn. She was suddenly caught up in the action and she liked it. It made her feel useful and somehow connected to Winn. She asked appropriate questions, made constructive suggestions, and when she was finally satisfied, she signed off on Dee's plans. She was kept so busy that she was no longer consumed by the urge to curl up and disappear, but there were times when she would close her eyes and pretend it was all a dream, and when she opened her eyes Winn would be standing there.

Less than an hour after the assassination, a lab coated forensic team from the FBI swarmed over the Senator's room. They wore white booties over their shoes and tight-fitting surgical gloves on their hands. Two of them swabbed at his remains, respectfully speaking to him as if he were still alive. They inserted something that looked like a meat thermometer into his open belly and jotted down the time of death. A third man was scooping up particles from the room and the balcony, placing them into plastic bags and marking them with labels. The local coroner was told he could watch but not touch anything until they said so.

A team from the National Transportation Agency arrived and headed for the crash site. More forensics agents from the FBI joined them and they were huddling to determine who would do what. The hill was covered with ash and remnants of metal. There was a partially intact blade that had been catapulted into the valley below but the mark on the blade was indecipherable. The explosion had incinerated the pilot. The area was roped off and the crash scene investigation began.

In the living room, two FBI agents and a CIA operative were interviewing Charles and the other servants to see if they might have seen something that would be helpful. Secret Service agents were hanging around leaning against the walls. They were waiting for someone to tell them what they were supposed to do, who they were supposed to protect, but until the orders came down they would just keep leaning against the wall.

Duke Connelly stuck his nose into the room and was told to stand by but not to interfere. The Chief fumed but tried not to show it. He would just be affable and patient for now and bide his time until the press conference. It wouldn't be long before the public knew his name and recognized his face. His days of being invisible were almost over.

Chapter 12

Griff was on the alert as they passed through the mountainous Victorian town of Cumberland, but as they got further into the Allegheny Mountains near Pittsburgh, he let himself nod off. Awakened for a rest stop in Cleveland, he went into the convenience store to buy a snack, but he broke into a cold sweat when he walked by the refrigerated case that displayed his favorite beers, Yuengling, Sam Adams, Heineken.

Just seeing the beer made his mouth begin to water, to want to taste it, to begin to crave it. He reminded himself that he had better think of the consequences of that first gulp; that he had better recite the mantra. He couldn't let this stress push him off the wagon because this time it wasn't only his problem, but it was also a problem for all those countless other people who didn't even know they were depending on him. His legs felt like stumps of lead, but he managed to turn his back to the cold case, put one footstep in front of the other and get back on the bus. Just a normal act for most people but a victorious one for him!

Still, by the time he found his seat, he was shivering. True, he had racked up another win; one more time he had conquered his craving and crushed the monster. He should have felt relieved but calm eluded him. His mind kept racing. Racing back to the bad times. Sometimes he couldn't remember their faces, but he could still feel the piercing pain of their goodbyes. Winn's death brought it all back. He was grateful that he was a captive on the highway, securely locked inside this metal box nowhere near a beckoning bar; mercifully protected from the magnetic pull of nothingness. He wished this machine would just keep on going so he could postpone his appointment with reality forever. He wanted to be somebody else. He tried to formulate a plan but nothing came to him. All he could see was a dark hole.

The bus rode steadily across the rich, black soil of Indiana, past its rivers and lakes and through the gently rolling hills surrounding the city of South Bend. Once more, Griff surrendered to the steady hum and movement of the bus, and he fell into a twilight sleep.

It was 2 o'clock in the morning when the bus finally pulled into one of the bays in the grimy Greyhound Bus Station on the Southside near the Chicago Loop. He had no idea where to go or what to do to hide from the dangers he imagined were lurking in the shadows of this night. His brain was frozen in time, his normally creative mind numbed by the events of the past day. At the same time, he knew he couldn't shirk his responsibilities to Winn, to himself, to the untold number of people who were all of a sudden his job to protect. Winn would tell him to pull himself together and be smart. That was his plan.

Finding a place to park in the middle of the night was the first order of business. From the bus station, he could see a Holiday Inn less than a block away, and he headed in that direction. He thought he heard footsteps following him, but soon he realized that they were his own squishy sneakers. Still, he was relieved to reach the hotel entrance. He would have to invent some story about having no ID, but he figured a night clerk would take cash to look the other way. He wouldn't flash enough cash to call attention to himself but just enough to get a room for the night.

The hotel was old and the lobby had seen better days. A sleazy looking desk clerk, who was half asleep and cranky at being interrupted by a late night intruder, manned the front desk. He asked for a credit card. Griff explained that his wallet had disappeared during his travels; he'd either lost it or someone had taken it, but he had stashed some money in another pocket, and he could pay cash. The clerk shrugged, tacked on a $20.00 surcharge, which he probably pocketed, and Griff paid the rack rate plus the $20.00 without feeling the need to tip him. He signed the register James Kennedy, which simply popped into his head as a nondescript Irish name to go with his typical Irish face. The clerk must have clocked him as a loser who wouldn't complain, and he gave him the cardkey to a rundown single room on the second floor overlooking the garbage bin.

"Check out by eleven or bring cash down here to pay for another day. Ya hear, fella?"

"Yes sir. No problem." replied Griff, thinking to himself how scruffy clothes, the stubble of a beard, and a middle-of-the-night appearance in a shabby hotel had reduced him in the eyes of the desk clerk to the lower ranks of the human race, at least one rung beneath the clerk's.

First thing tomorrow Griff would figure out how to get the word out. He thought he had at least 24 hours left but he couldn't guarantee the enemy wouldn't move faster. He gathered up some tourist maps and brochures from a rack in the lobby and took the fire stairs to his room.

The room had a sour smell that gagged him when he first entered. So this is how others live, he thought to himself, people he would likely never meet in his cocoon of a world. The bedspread was stained and the mattress sagged in the middle. There was a tiny sink in the room with a slow and steady drip that formed a brown stain around the drain. An old claw-footed tub and a dark stained toilet completed his accommodations, and he peed in the toilet because he needed to and made circles in the bowl just to break the tension. He looked around for roaches, but he didn't see any. Maybe he'd caught a break in the roach department.

How did it come to this? One guy in a dingy room trying to figure out how to save the world! But that is what it came down to, and he would have face up to the challenge and get on with it.

He spread out the maps and the brochures on the worn dresser and figured out that the Chicago campus of the University of Illinois was within easy walking distance. There were Internet wireless hookups just about everywhere – the University library, Starbucks, bookstores around the campus, but he had no laptop, and it was too problematic for him to buy one on the legal market. In one of the brochures, he located a combination laundromat and Internet café near the University where he wouldn't need his own computer, but he decided to try the University first.

He soaked in the tub, got a little shut-eye, grabbed his stuff, left for the campus at 8 AM, and with the help of the University map, he located the library. He bought a breakfast bar from the vending machine in the lounge and slipped into the main room. Students were working at tables, tapping away on their laptops. There were two unmanned desktops, one sitting on either side of a square table. One was turned off the other was logged in as if it were waiting for Griff. No one around seemed to be using it. This was the break he needed. Thank you, God!

Despite the anxiety he was feeling, Griff chuckled. His parents would be amazed and happy to hear him invoke the name of the Almighty. He hadn't done that since he was an alter boy. In fact, the only times he'd been inside a church for the past twenty years was for funerals and weddings, and he avoided them whenever he could. If this worked out though, he would like to make it back to Winn's send-off. Maybe that would help dissolve the lump in his throat that wouldn't go away.

He uploaded his memory chip to Sally's email, sent her a text message and took off for the nearest Fed Ex. Just in case he bit the dust or the email and the text message were somehow lost in space, he made one more hard copy of the press release. He overnighted it to Sally's attention at the Washington Post, mailed a certified copy of the names that required Sally's signature for delivery, and walked out into the sunlight finally daring to take a breath.

If all hell broke loose he needed to be in motion. If they tracked the chip he had to be long gone. He had to stay alive at least until he spoke to Sally or until he was sure the names were delivered. He and Winn had wanted these rats rolled up before they knew they had been fingered. They had planned to use Winn's high security clout to issue the Senate subpoenas that Griff had prepared despite the fact that there had been no time to clear them! In D.C. the Sergeant-at-Arms would serve them together with a covey of Capitol policemen who would make the arrests. Griff had made arrangements with the City jail to hold them until Court approved FBI subpoenas could be obtained. The arrests were intended to go down fast and get legal later.

In New York, a CIA operative, a longtime friend of Griff's, who only knew that subpoenas would be emailed and that this was something Ainsley had personally requested, would pick up the three UN culprits ad hoc and hold them until further instructions. Griff assured him he would be protected. Now that this plan was caput, Griff was depending on Sally to come to the rescue. He had done all he could do for now. Now, it was a waiting game.

Griff thought about the choices he'd made in the early years and in a fleeting flash of the self-pity that had almost done him in, he wished he'd taken that cushy job in a top Washington law firm right out of law school. He had gone to work for Winn instead because he believed that

Winn had that rare quality of greatness, and until the last, Winn had never shaken that belief. Winn had been there for Griff when booze became his lord and master. He had picked him up out of the gutter, cleaned him up and convinced him to get into a treatment facility. Without Winn's faith in him he would probably have drunk himself into oblivion. He owed Winn for his life, and he owed him for a career that was a perfect fit for his considerable talents. With Winn, Griff could stay behind the scenes where he was most comfortable, and he could make big things happen through Winn's voice. Together, they were an unbeatable team.

Having just gone through trial by fire, Griff gained a little bit of confidence that he could handle the future. Through all the unbearable tension of the past two days, he had discovered a deep reservoir of inner strength. Despite the baggage of the bad years, his old true self, the one that made him high school senior class president and college valedictorian, had somehow survived.

Chapter 13

Sally regularly checked her email. Griff's immediately caught her eye. She read it in disbelief and knew it was a big deal. He told her the White House had been compromised; they had to trust someone, and the President seemed to be the safest choice. Could she get to him through her one-time buddy, the President's personal secretary, without showing her hand? He would give her an hour and then check in.

Griff hopped on the L, got off close to a Target he had scoped out, bought two disposable cells and headed for Grant Park. At the entrance, he bought an all-beef Chicago style hot dog off a busy chuck wagon. It was served up on the traditional Chicago poppy seed bun, slathered with yellow mustard and spread with lots of sweet pickle relish. He found a park bench on the lakefront, wolfed down the dog and went back for seconds.

Time went by slowly, but he wanted to have only one conversation with Sally on this cell, so he waited and at the one-hour mark, he called. Her voice got to him, and he choked up with an emotion he hadn't known he was capable of. He didn't know what it was but it was strong.

"Griff, are you okay?"

"I'll do for now." She told him she had tried to set up the meeting through her erstwhile friend, but she finally needed Feld's clout to arrange it.

The meeting with the President was set up for 7 o'clock that evening in the Residence. Griff read off the names to Sally and she recorded them in longhand. Now the timeline was in better shape. Score one for the good guys! " I need help to get back fast, Sally, but I'd feel better if we can keep it under the radar. I'll get back to you later, somewhere around 9. See what you can do, but be careful. Keep the circle tight."

"Griff, please stay safe. I'll work this end, but you have got to stay safe."

"Will do. Catch you later."

A great sense of relief washed over him, not only because he had passed on the names, but also because Sally's velvet voice had calmed him. He walked past the big fountain toward the jogging path, and when he got to a place close enough to the Lake, he tossed the cell.

Chapter 14

Feld came by for Sally in his long black limo. His driver opened the door for her, and she slid in gracefully, emulating the ladylike way she had learned on her way up the ladder – first putting her hindquarter down on the seat and then putting her legs together and swinging them in one motion onto the car floor. It took concentration at first, but it was second nature to her now.

Feld and Sally conferred on the best way to present this to the President, who would cover which facts, how much detail they needed to provide and went over the handout they would leave with him. Sally had prepared one page with bullets, and a second page with the culprits' names printed in longhand. Just as Griff had directed, she had made no electronic record.

Feld was courteous and friendly. "He is a nice man." Sally thought, and wondered why he had a reputation for being such a hard-nosed guy. Thank goodness he had a good relationship with the President, and thank goodness he had recognized the need for crisis mode. They were expected and the guards at the White House gate handed them their badges. The driver was told to drop them off at the West Portico and to park in a specific spot to wait for them. Secret Service agents, who escorted them in and showed them to the elevator that would take them to the Residence, met them at the Portico. An agent greeted them as they got off the elevator and escorted them up the ramp to the Solarium, which was a cozy retreat, very different from the formality of the rest of the living quarters. It was the President's favorite hideaway, a place where he could remove his shoes, mix his own drink, and even prepare a peanut butter and jelly sandwich in the kitchenette away from the angry glare of his chef or the playful ridicule of his wife.

President Amos Jackson was a complicated man. He was raised in the progressive heart of Wisconsin, in Madison where his father taught political science at the University, and his mother taught math at the local high school. His father, a utopian thinker who believed that the use of military force was an indefensible failure of diplomacy and that the root-cause of all third-world aggression was poverty, had written several books on terrorism, one of which, "In the Eye of the Beholder" was considered essential reading for any political science major. His mother, who kept her politics private, was a pretty woman but stern and reserved. It seemed to Amos that her lips were perpetually parsed, and other than a brief hug and pat on the shoulder at his high school and college graduations, he could not remember an affectionate moment.

On the other hand, his father was demonstrative to the point of embarrassment, and Amos cringed at his frequent displays of affection, especially those he indulged in when Amos' buddies were around. Whenever his father hugged his mother she became a statue, and Amos wondered how in the world he was conceived. Both of his parents seemed indifferent to religious practices, but his father told him bible stories at bedtime, and they all dutifully went to the University Chapel on Christmas Eve and Easter. Christmas Day was the only festive time in his childhood home, mainly because his father invited all of his students to come by for non-alcoholic eggnog and a nice food spread of salads and hefty sandwiches. His mother made the salads, and his father bought the popular sandwiches ready-made from a nearby German delicatessen. It was Amos' favorite day of the year.

Amos met his wife Betsy during their law school days at Duke, and after that, North Carolina became his home. Betsy, a tomboy with an athletic build, a pretty soap-scrubbed face, and a permanent smile that crinkled her eyes and dimpled her cheeks, was one of five kids, the oldest and only sister in a household of raucous, sports loving younger brothers. Her parents were a friendly and outgoing pair whose idea of a fun day was motor home tailgating at a college football game beginning at eight in the morning and ending only after the game was over or the sun went down, whichever came first. They opened their arms to him from the first, and he fell in love with them as much as with Betsy. It was a package deal he never failed to appreciate.

Most of Betsy's family members were Republicans, the kind that were labeled compassionate conservatives by the old Bush dynasty. They were church going and charitable, served up Thanksgiving or Christmas dinner to the homeless, visited the sick and aged, and pulled weeds in the church yard. They believed in giving a hand-up to those who were down on their luck, supported only those government programs that led to individual independence and opposed programs they considered handouts. They believed that government's chief responsibility was to provide security and were staunch supporters of the fire and police departments and of the military.

Amos and Betsy led a charmed life except for the fact that they were not able to have children. In the early years they spoke of adopting but as Amos' political life took off and consumed their days, they just stopped talking about it.

Amos ran for President as an Independent in a day when the political parties were in profound disfavor. After decades of waffling, trying this remedy or that remedy, voting for catchy slogans such as "change you can believe in," or "real change," or "common sense government," or "experience matters," or "a government that works," or "character counts," the voters finally rejected the poisonous partisanship, insidious corruption and all-consuming self-interest and greed that were pervasive on both sides of the aisle of the nation's Capitol. Honest

Amos, a moderate Democrat who had earned a sterling reputation as an incorruptible centrist in the North Carolina legislature and then as its competent governor for eight years, was overwhelmingly elected President on an Independent Party Unity ticket. He made a campaign commitment to bring leaders of both parties, experts from academia, and the cream of the crop from government, finance, industry, think tanks and other non-profits into his Cabinet and into the White House, and he conscientiously kept his word.

Mostly, Amos was a pragmatist who by and large tried to figure out how to blend differing opinions to get a good result. A skilled compromiser, he believed that half a loaf was better than none, and he was willing to accept the small steps that would, over time, get him to the finish line. His job, he thought, was to leave high office with his fellow Americans and the world community safer and better off than they were when he came in. He quickly learned the institutional ways of the Congress and was talented at applying the levers of power not too hard but just hard enough to move a piece of legislation through it. Although he had accumulated an abundance of untainted chits, he salted away as many IOUs as he could for a moment that really mattered. Possessed of an uncanny ability to understand the human strengths and human weaknesses of each of his allies and opponents, he used this insight to gently prod them to his side. So far his accomplishments as President were many, and his enemies still few.

A big man, tall and muscular with a craggy face reminiscent of Lincoln but better looking, he laughed heartily, cried without shame and somehow owned every room he entered. He was a spinner of yarns, a spellbinding storyteller who held his listeners in the palm of his hand, but he was also a serious man who cared deeply for his fellow man. He never felt above them but one of them, and it was this humility that was his most endearing quality.

Chapter 15

The President greeted Feld and Sally with an extended hand and offered drinks and some munchies that were sitting on the cocktail table. They accepted the drinks, which the President fixed in the kitchenette, and then he motioned for them to sit in the lounge chairs opposite the sofa. In stocking feet, Amos spread out on the sofa, folded his arms behind his head and said, "This is one hell of an awful thing that's happened to Winn. What can you tell me about it?"

Feld and Sally chronicled the facts without embellishment, like the incisive reporters Feld once had been and Sally still was. Sally handed the President the two pages she'd brought. Amos read them twice, and he turned pale. Heavy silence hung in the room. No one spoke for what seemed to be an eternity. He sat up, punched a number on his hard line, gave a brief order, put on his shoes and suggested they have another drink. He poured and said he wanted them to stick around.

Then all hell broke loose. Suddenly the sunroom was filled with people. The President was a picture of calm. His voice was steady and clear and his instructions were precise. Each person left with no doubt about his or her mission. The wheels were in motion.

Griff called Sally on his second cell. The President got on the line, directed him to go to Scott Air Force base at O'Hare where he would be met and where there would be a plane waiting to take him to Andrews.

Between nine and eleven o'clock that evening, Friday, August 15, 2026, ten people, nine men and one woman, were simultaneously rolled up from their homes, their neighborhood bars and their cocktail parties and were being held incommunicado in various places. The Attorney

General was busy developing the rationale to hold them. The President told him that he would personally take the heat if it was a problem, but there was no way they would be remanded to anyone or anyplace else without his order.

As the first order of business the energy codes were scrambled, and the President directed that they be monitored 24/7 and changed on an irregular schedule for now. He wanted some expertise brought in fast to provide foolproof ways to secure them and to develop a failsafe backup system. He wanted a review of the vetting process. How the hell did these vermin get clearance in the first place? How did they penetrate the codes? Were there any more loose canons floating around? He wanted answers.

Amos asked Sally and Feld to stay for dinner. He said, "I have more to do, and I think you will enjoy listening. I'm about to break the rules, but I have the feeling I can trust you not to spill the beans. You've got plenty of meat already."

Sally and Feld were more than happy to comply. As much as they had respected this man, they were now totally enamored of him. Feld and Sarah were due at synagogue services that Friday night, and he called Sarah to make sure that she explained to the rabbi that he was delayed, nothing more.

Dinner was a simple affair – filet of beef with a mushroom glaze, a baked sweet potato with cinnamon and butter, huge tender asparagus, and crusty French rolls. Before dinner, the President had thoughtfully asked Feld if the meal met with his dietary restrictions. Feld replied that he and Sarah kept kosher at home but it was too daunting for him to try to be kosher out on the Washington circuit. Feld chuckled, " Sarah is careful not to ask too much, and I am careful not to tell too much." The dinner table repartee continued in a light vein.

The President's favorite dessert, lemon meringue pie, was being served when his National Security Advisor, former Howard University International Studies provost, Molly Bentsen, came in with a tentative smile on her face. She felt she needed to try to redeem herself after two of her people, people she had hand picked, men she had trusted with sensitive information, were guilty of such dastardly acts. But on a more realistic level she believed she would have to go and later she would let the President know that she was okay with it. She just hoped it could be done in a way that would not demolish her career.

She sat down at the table and said, "It's been set up, Mr. President. There is a discreet cordon around the Iranian Embassy and one around the Saudi Embassy. I have Iranian President Farid Zahedi on the line, sir."

"Amos Jackson here. How are you doing Mr. President? You and I, we have a little problem we have to solve here. We sure don't want to make it a bigger problem than it needs to be, do we? You've got two men in your Embassy who are doing some very bad stuff. Now, I'm sure they are acting on their own. We got some rotten apples in our barrel, too. We're bringing our bad guys in as we speak. After Ainsley's murder, Mr. President, my people are out for blood. I got to throw some meat to those bloodhounds, you know. I got some men waiting outside your Embassy gate, just waiting to take your bad guys in. We'll keep them for a while, shine the spotlight on them, and then arrange to hand them off to you. That'll solve my problem, and it'll help you solve yours. We arrest the bad guys, and you're off the hook. We make a joint statement expressing our shared contempt for their action; our mutual resolve to see these criminals brought to justice and our determination to continue to explore our economic relationship. We can't take them in until you shove them out the Embassy gate. What do you say, Farid?"

The American President smiled as he listened to the Iranian President stutter. Then he said, "Thanks, Farid. Our people will be in touch tonight to set up a videoconference for our joint statement. Goodnight, now."

"You got King Khalid on the line, Molly?" She nodded and said, "Yes sir, Mr. President. He agreed to wait as long as he has to. He's being very cooperative, sir.

"Your Highness, Amos Jackson here. We have a little problem. There's a guy named Abdullah al Omari who works in your Embassy. He is a big troublemaker, sir. He's creating a bad situation for us, and a bad situation for the Kingdom. I know you must be upset with his disgraceful behavior, and we'd like to help you out. If you give him a little shove out the Embassy gate, we'll deal with him, twist him in the wind for a while to satisfy our folks and then hand him off to you. That'll solve our predicament. You and I have a meeting scheduled next month when we are supposed to make that joint announcement on the Nighthawk sale, and we don't want a bureaucrat like Abdullah to spoil it for the both of us. You get him out the gate within the hour and my people will pick it up from there. Can I count on you?"

The President listened, and then said, "Your Highness, you are a wise man and I knew you would understand our dilemma. I'm looking forward to our meeting next month. Our people will be getting together soon to work up an agenda we can both live with. Please give my warm regards to your nephew, Prince Nayif. I met him a few weeks ago, and I am looking forward to seeing him again. Goodnight, now."

"Molly, we have to work out the diplomatic immunity thing. We've got to string up those Embassy guys publicly before we can ship them home. They have to take some heavy heat. As far as our own people are concerned, they can't see the light of day for a long time. Do it as carefully as you can. Dot the Is, cross the Ts, make sure Justice stays on it but don't let them out of our custody. I'll be the lightning rod if I have to be, but I have the feeling we're going to have plenty of support on this. If the ACLU types come wringing their hands and moralizing the due process issues, have them meet with Justice and then the CIA director. If they can't get them to understand our outrage at Ainsley's assassination, I'll see them next."

"Where are we on the Saudi Nighthawk sale, Molly?"

"Sir, I'll check on the latest but as far as I know, its still in Committee."

"How about we keep it there? Get one of our friends on the Committee to exercise personal privilege. No fingerprints. That will buy us time to have State and Defense find some technical reasons to withdraw their approvals and call off the financing. Let Boeing know we'll make it up to them. And, Molly, look, we've got our supply bases in Kuwait and Qatar, boots and flyover rights in Iraq, more Arab allies on board squeezing Iran, our 5th fleet in the Gulf, and a mighty Israel on our left flank. We've got a big enough footprint to keep things cool there so why the hell are we still arming the Saudis? They've lost their oil leverage. They haven't made any honest attempt to restructure their government, and they haven't done a damn thing to reform their Wahabbi madrassas, and God knows, the students in those madrassas are still swaying to the tune of 'Death to America.' We can at least get a little linkage going here."

"Make no mistake, Molly, for the Saudi and Iranian governments; this is just a temporary setback. They will keep trying to come at us one way or another, but right now they are so strapped for money, they probably can't do much. We know that the Saudi Royals will let go of their iron grip only when they have no other choice, and Iran's fervor to crush the West and wipe Israel off the map won't cool down easy, either.

We have to keep reminding Iran, Molly, that our eyes in the sky are keeping a close watch on the new nuclear facility they say they're not building near Natanz and that the missile shield technology we've developed with Israel can handle anything they've got. I don't think the use of a nuclear weapon would bother them in the least. It would just fit into their narrative of the end of days. You would think that with their economies in the ditch, the Saudis and the Iranians would want to join their enlightened Arab neighbors. Except for them, the region has leapfrogged into modernity. They have accepted co-existence with Israel and the West, embraced free trade, welcomed investment, and they are prospering and moving towards more open and democratic societies."

"Even though we could argue the merits forever, our show of American strength and persistence in Iraq moved the pendulum just enough to change the nasty dynamics of that region. The outcome gave us a staunch ally in our efforts to contain Iran; it met the strategic necessity of protecting the region's resources from Saddam's hostile ambitions, and it brought freedom to the 26 million captive Iraqis who were caught up in Saddam's bloody chokehold. We know the Arab world respects strength, and they sat back for a while to see if we had the guts to stick it out. If the new look of the region is a marker, we passed the test. Now, our relationships in that part of the globe are solid, except for those two stubborn holdouts."

"As for the Iranian people, they are speaking out loud and clear on the economic package that we're dangling on the Hill, and we hear them, but we've got to have a verifiable agreement with their leaders on the nukes first. It's the only leverage we've got. In the end, I believe Iran's Ayatollahs and their hard line political leaders will push too hard and be hoisted up on their own petards. The people are educated and eager to follow western ways. Too bad they have suffered so many failed attempts to overthrow the regime, but sooner or later they will win out. I'm less optimistic about the Saudis. They remain insular, too isolated from the reality of life outside their closed borders. Only so much we can do there until a new generation of leaders embraces modernity and the people decide to follow them. With Israel peacefully co-existing with a young Palestinian State, the convenient excuse for radicalism is off the table. The Iranians can't feed terrorists with oil money that's disappearing. The same deal applies to the Saudis and their madrassas. The tide will engulf these holdouts if they don't come around soon."

Amos tilted his chair back, folded his hands behind his head as he often did when he was mulling things over and said, "Back to the business at hand. We've got to have something positive come out of this tragedy, Molly. I want you to set up a study group charged with making recommendations to avoid a repeat performance. Bring in the usual players and make sure the DIA boys are included. They will give me a consensus report I can fall back on if I need to, but I want an independent report too. Put together a second group that's loaded with superstars who are sure to end up butting heads. I'll get at least two reports from them, and maybe we'll see some fresh thinking. Just make sure they understand I expect them to be honest with each other, close mouthed about their deliberations, and civil enough to refrain from backstabbing when they leave the building. A tall order for sure, but you just sweet talk them, Molly, and keep them on course."

"Tomorrow morning I'll pull together the key staffers who can give you the help you'll need on this. We need to keep Congress informed. We need to email them 'til they scream uncle, and we need to bring in the leaders and the key chairmen for briefing sessions in addition to the weekly meetings I have with them now. Run your list by me."

As Molly got her papers together and prepared to leave, Amos said, "By the way, Molly, I can imagine how hard this has been on you. Don't sweat it for now. Let's see how the chips fall before you jump to any conclusions. Okay?"

"Feld, I am going to call Prime Minister Posner to see if he has any advice on handling this nightmare. I want to find out if the Mossad picked up any noise that makes more sense now. Maybe they can help us figure out who fingered Winn. And Feld, I'm going to keep you in the loop. I owe you."

"Off the record, there is going to be an announcement in the next few months on our efforts to pull together a global environmental initiative that brings in India and China in lead roles. I'll have my people send some briefing papers over to you for background so you'll be ready to go on short notice. You will be the first to get the green light."

As soon as Feld and Sally got into the limo, he phoned his wife. "I'm on my way home, Sarah. What did you tell the rabbi? Fine. I'll explain tomorrow. Don't bother. I already had dinner. I'll see you in twenty minutes. Goodbye, sweetheart."

Sally pinched herself. Yesterday, she was just a hard-driving working girl. Today, she was a witness to history, a middleman in a conspiracy that reached across the globe, a messenger of critical information that swept up a nest of spies, a go-between for Griff's safe return, a dinner guest at the President's residence and a passenger in Feld's limo.

She was an insider now, but she would work hard to see that she never ended up "in the tank." It was a delicate balance and she would have to keep a critical eye on her work. She couldn't digest all of this at once. Her head was spinning and she just wanted to go home.

Feld said he wanted to talk to her on Monday morning at 8:30. He dropped her off and waited at the curb until she was safely inside.

Sally kicked off her boots at the front door, put the TV on an all-news, all-night channel, and fell across the bed in her clothes. She told herself she would take them off soon and shower. Instead, she fell sound asleep until the bright slanted rays of the morning sun awakened her.

Chapter 16

In the mystifying pathways of cyberspace, frantic exchanges were burning the airwaves. From Riyadh to Tehran, from Tehran to Riyadh, from Tehran to the Iranian embassy on Belmont Road, and from Riyadh to the Saudi embassy on New Hampshire Avenue, there was scurrying and shouting intermingled with Persian poetry and Arab pronouncements of righteous indignation.

"The Great Satan has won this skirmish, but in the end Allah shall put our souls into green birds and fly us to the rivers of Paradise." said Zahedi. "Allah, blessed be his name, has fated that you and I and our people shall be together in the kingdom of heaven. We shall be martyrs for Islam, and we shall share rivers of wine, dark-eyed virgins, and respectful servant boys."

"These upstart Americans; they do not know their place. We are an ancient people, the best of peoples, and we shall win in the end. Inshallah." said the King. "We must find the informant. He is an apostate and he must be punished by the sword."

"There is also a matter of business," said Zahedi "We must change the traffic channels for the Alliance for Mid-East Peace and Prosperity. Our contact tells us that the Americans have found a way to track the money, and we must find a safer means to put our hands in their pockets. Peace be upon you."

"Allah hu Akbar. "Allah hu Akbar."

"Ash-hadu an-la, Ila-ha illallah

God is great. God is great.

I bear witness there is no God but God."

At O'Hare, Golden Eagle 12, the newest Air Force jet and the pride and joy of the Air National Guard Unit at Scott, was fueled and ready to take off as soon as Griff rolled up to the gate. A cadre of uniformed men and a Secret Service team of four met him and immediately escorted him to the runway and up the movable stairs. He had removed his gold earrings and wore a long sleeved tee shirt to conceal his serpent tattoo. He looked scruffy but normal.

Inside, the plane was outfitted for the brass with comfortable tan leather lounge chairs surrounding a long oval conference table. He was led to a seat at the head of the table where a hot gourmet meal was waiting for him. An attractive female flight attendant in an Air National Guard uniform wheeled a full bar to him and asked what he would like to drink. The lead agent said Griff had sure earned a stiff drink. Griff said he was looking forward to a good dinner, but he'd just like a ginger ale though it wouldn't bother him if they chose the booze. He said he knew they needed to debrief him, and they could begin whenever they chose. He was ready.

They landed at Andrews at 4 AM; Griff was taken in a military caravan directly to Camp David where the comfortable guest cabin, the Dogwood, was ready and waiting. Dawn was breaking as they reached the retreat. Bright patches of early sunlight flickered their way through the stately oaks and poplars that lined the winding roadway. As they rounded a sharp curve, orchards of wild cherry trees past their prime came into view and splashed the mossy green valley below with clusters of faded crimson blossoms. President Franklin Delano Roosevelt chose this magnificent enclave in the Catoctin Mountains for rest and relaxation, and for a sociable place for high-level meetings away from the din and distractions of the nation's Capitol. With Roosevelt's blessing, it was named Shangri-La after British author James Hilton's mystical kingdom, and although its name had changed, it remained an earthly paradise isolated from the outside world. Surrounded by beauty and quiet, Griff began to relax.

Major General Dickey Ames who was assigned to Griff opened the cabin door and handed him an old-fashioned key. There was a terry robe and a change of clothes on the bed, and he gave Griff a cell.

"Call me on 6 when you're ready, and we'll continue the debriefing at the Communications Center. It's just up the main road to your left. This place is pretty compact and you can't miss it. The President and the First Lady came up for the weekend so you may just cross paths. I'm usually part of his detail, and I can tell you from personal experience that he is a great guy. Puts up with pomp and circumstance because he has to, but up here he can just be himself. Address him as Mr. President because it's custom but be loose."

"If it's okay with you, I'd like to call Sally Burton"

"Not yet," Ames replied. "An intervening conversation could interfere with your first hand account of what transpired. It won't be long. Let's discuss it again after today's meeting."

"Damn," Griff thought to himself. "I need to hear her voice again." Since the phone call, he had thought of her incessantly. He couldn't shake the velvet voice.

Chapter 17

The funeral was set for Wednesday, August 19 at 10 o'clock in the morning at the National Cathedral. The President and the First Lady were seated to Celeste's right and Charles to her left. Charles was reluctant, told Celeste he felt it was inappropriate for a servant to sit by her, but she would have none of it. Charles had been a constant and calming presence since Winn's death, and she wanted him by her side so she could cope with the emotional rollercoaster of the service. She knew cameras were everywhere, and she wanted to appear like the Rock of Gibraltar when she actually felt so delicate that she thought she could easily break into a thousand little pieces. But when she glanced at Charles for support he was there for her, and she felt better.

The Cathedral was filled to capacity. Dee made sure that Winn's send-off would be stately and respectful and that its ceremonial words would elevate this honorable man to the status of national hero. The President felt that the nation owed this tribute to Winn and got directly involved to make sure that the tone was just right. Betsy had accompanied Dee to Celeste's home on two occasions when she offered to personally lend a hand to Celeste in any way she could. Betsy's compassion came through loud and clear, and Celeste broke down and cried on her shoulder. She helped Celeste go through her closets to select outfits for the Rotunda ceremony and for the funeral. A warm bond of sisterhood was sealed during that difficult time, a rare friendship that would last long after the official bonds were broken.

Griff was seated in the front row with Sally beside him. Arranged by the President as a total surprise for Griff, Sally had appeared at Camp David on Sunday evening at the dinner table. Griff's shaved head took

Sally by surprise and she blurted out, "Griff, are you having a mid-life crisis or what? Oh, my gosh, are those earring holes?"

"Yes, those are earring holes. On the mid-life crisis, I take the Fifth."

After a casual dinner of chicken potpie and chocolate bread pudding, the President said he was turning in early, thanked both Sally and Griff for all they had done, and he and Betsy parted hand in hand.

Sally and Griff strolled at a snail's pace towards their cabins, which were situated next to each other. There was an awkward moment, but Griff couldn't let this day end yet and he said, "How about we talk in my cabin?" Until then, except for a kiss on the cheek they hadn't touched. From the first instant they were alone, he had this physically powerful urge to reach out and pull her into his arms, but he wasn't sure how she would react, and he didn't want to mess up their friendship.

Still, a voice inside told him he needed to take the risk. Over and over again, he had let the past tear down the present. He had allowed the hovering ghosts of yesterday block his path. He had pushed aside his feelings for Sally for so long but no more. He wanted to deal with them.

Sally didn't want the day to end either. When Griff was in danger, she felt a strong impulse to rescue him. She had come to depend on those frequent dinners with Griff, on the comforting sight of Griff showing up on Fridays; Griff sitting out on the patio with his root beer; Griff highlighting the tableau of her private life. She couldn't imagine Friday nights without him. She didn't want to.

It happened quite naturally. No subterfuge. No silly maneuvers. In magical union, they fell into each other's arms conscious only of the melting of their flesh and the rhythms of their heartbeat fusing into one another. The walls they had built crumbled and disappeared in the lightning bolt of mind-blowing flashes that surpassed even their most sensual dreams. At that earth-shaking moment, neither could distinguish whose tremors they were feeling, whose hot skin they were touching, whose lips were quivering, whose pulse was pounding, where one ended and the other began.

When Sally caught her breath, she asked, "Griff, is all of this real? Or am I dreaming? It's such a beautiful dream, Griff, please don't wake me up."

"It's real, Sally. By God, it's real."

Although both of them had known it for a long time, they had been too terrified to admit that they belonged together. They tried to make up for lost time until Sally had to roll out of bed to keep her appointment with Feld.

Chapter 18

The last of the Ainsleys was laid to rest at Arlington Cemetery under a spreading oak tree that seemed to be lifting its arms in protest to the heavens from which came the fatal blow. United States Senator Winston Ainsley was lowered into a patch of hallowed ground near fellow Senators and distinguished American heroes whose names are honored in history. Celeste reflected that he would have especially liked that he was placed not far from the monument that stood in tribute to the unknown soldiers who had fought and died for their country and whose absent names were known only to God.

Unable to provide Winn the happiness he craved during their life together, Celeste was now content that she had done the best she could for him in death. The Senate Chaplain spoke of Winn's strength and of his enduring devotion to his country and with no cameras at the gravesite, Celeste could finally weep.

A small and sad group of those who had been at graveside accompanied Celeste to Laurelwood where there was a food buffet, wine and muted conversation. Each in turn offered their condolences to Celeste and in a little while, they were gone. Only Charles remained.

Celeste wandered through the stately rooms of the mansion that now seemed so empty, so frightening. When he had inquired, she had informed the Governor that she was not interested in filling the remainder of Winn's term. Somehow she knew she had to come to terms with her past. This house had brought her no peace, no escape from her tortured memories, no real happiness. It had provided only a shell in which she could hide. She needed to find out if there was more, and she didn't think she could do that if she remained at Laurelwood.

Over the next days Celeste asked herself again and again why she had remained in this place so haunted by walls that knew her shameful secrets. The sound of her bedroom door opening and then the click of the lock! The silent scream she still heard in her nightmares. Her father whom she had adored, doing unspeakable things to her! Warning her to remain silent, that no one would believe her. Then, the arguments! Her father shouting! Her mother sobbing!

It was at the breakfast table the day following each episode that Celeste learned to build her shell. Her father would be reading the newspaper, her mother chatting as if nothing had happened, the two of them occasionally exchanging a comment or two, going over the day's schedule, discussing an upcoming party they were planning, asking Celeste if she had finished her homework, all very normal.

And then that awful night when Winn had had too much to drink! Celeste refused his rough advances, and he ignored her. First, he was insistent, then he was unstoppable and Celeste snapped. Winn's face suddenly became her father's face, his groping hands became her father's hands, his whiskey breath became her father's breath and his forceful thrusting became her father's thrusting. Celeste tried to push him away; she begged him to stop, but her struggle seemed to excite him even more.

She had to kill the pain; she had to kill the memories. Suddenly, the tiny pistol she kept under her pillow was in her hand, and Winn wrested it from her with astonishment and deep sorrow. She couldn't remember reaching for it. She couldn't remember holding it. No matter how hard she tried, those life-changing moments remained a blank. But she did remember the pistol in his hand and the tragic look on his face. She never forgot that look.

The next morning, she had Charles move Winn's things to the guest wing, and they never spoke of it. Never! Just as her mother held so much inside, she continued the pattern. On more than one occasion, Winn tried to penetrate the wall she had erected, but Celeste couldn't bring herself to speak of the unspeakable. The old messages got in the way and she couldn't lose them. There were fleeting moments when she wanted to, but her moments were never in sync with his, and then Winn simply stopped trying.

Chapter 19

Floating on Cloud 9, Sally kept her appointment with Feld. Then Feld lifted her already high spirits even higher. He said, "For the past year, I've been keeping an eye on you, and I think you are ready to move up here. I like the way you manage your reporters. I like the balance you achieve in your columns. I like your nose for the big picture, your respect for facts and your eye for detail. You work smart, you work hard, and you're a go-getter. I don't know if you are aware of this but we share an alma mater. Columbia gave you strong news-hound bones, and I like to think that your years on this paper helped put good meat on them."

"Jake's wife is not well, and he wants to take her to their Florida home year-round. He doesn't want her to spend another winter here. After 35 years, I hate to lose him. The last ten years as my managing editor have been the best for both of us; he knows what I'm thinking before I do, and I know how he's going to react before he does, but he needs to retire and do the right thing for his wife. They will be leaving mid-December, and I'm asking you to shadow him until then, to learn the ropes, and then to work hard to try to fill his shoes. I will help you along the way if I think you need help or if you ask for it. It is not an easy job and you are still young, but I wouldn't ask if I didn't think you were up to it. What do you say?"

"I'm stunned," Sally replied. " I thought Jake would be here forever, and I never pictured myself in his job. I know I can never fill his shoes, but I also know that challenges don't scare me. I'd like to try, but I'd also like to spend some of my time in the next few months training my successor. I've worked hard to build the Style section, and I'd like to leave it in good hands. Sophie has filled in for me during my vacations, and she's good. I'd feel comfortable leaving things in her hands." She looked up, waiting for Feld's reaction.

"Set up a meeting with Jake, and work out the details. Feld stood, came around the desk, gave Sally a friendly pat on the shoulder, opened the door for her, and with a wide grin, he said, "We had quite a weekend, didn't we? One for the books!"

Sally just smiled and thought to herself, "You only know the half of it."

Chapter 20

Celeste scanned the real estate ads hoping they would lead her to the right agent. She chose Roberta Roberts, a middle-aged woman she had met on the party circuit, a chic and professional type who specialized in high-end properties. Roberta came to Laurelwood, looked things over with a critical eye and made suggestions that she felt would enhance the marketability of the property.

The beds at the front entry were now planted with all green shrubs, some old and too large, and Roberta thought that some new green scrubs, along with contrasting variegated and red plant material would be a nice touch against the all white exterior. She also suggested that seasonal flowers be added like garden jewelry, in small splashes of color carefully placed for a pleasing effect. She felt the house would be easier to market in the spring and didn't think it wise to list it until then. She would keep her eyes and ears open for potential buyers but since there was such a small universe of people who could afford this estate and she knew most of them, she trusted Celeste to sign up with her when the time was right.

Celeste made frequent visits to the local garden nursery. There, she found the long time owners eager not only to help with the selection of materials but also to describe the origin of each plant or flower, its scientific name and its common name, the type of soil in which it would thrive, the amount of sunlight that it preferred, when it would bloom and for how long, the flowers that attracted bees or butterflies, the plants that needed a mate, when to plant the different species, when to put in the spring bulbs, and on and on. They obviously loved what they were doing, and it made Celeste feel good just to be with them.

Celeste began to spend more time in the gardens. She learned to prune the roses, trim back the bushes, add proper nutrients to the different plant materials, turn over the beds, and pinch the flowers after they had bloomed. Each bed became a canvas, and the artistic talent that she hadn't known she possessed, began to shine. Time flew by when she was working in the gardens and even when her muscles ached and her bones rebelled, she would stop only when dusk approached and she knew it was time for a nice hot shower and dinner.

These days, Celeste ate all of her meals in the breakfast room. She couldn't bear Winn's empty dining room chair. It sat at the head of the table and the ghosts of memories past sat squarely in its seat.

At first she ate alone and Charles served her and ate in the kitchen after his serving duties were done. She asked Charles to keep her company, but he said he was a servant and it wasn't fitting. She reminded him that the inheritance he received from Winn, an investment portfolio that Winn had set up for him over fifteen years before, had grown to almost a million dollars. She teased him that he was financially able to quit his job and just be friends if that's what it took for him to join her for dinner and at the very least, to please call her Celeste. The good-natured sparring went on for months until Charles relented and they began to take their meals together. They ate either in the kitchen or in the breakfast room but never in the dining room where Winn's absence was still too keenly felt.

Charles began to help Celeste in the gardens. He bought a stack of gardening books, a couple of botany textbooks, and he became fascinated by the thousands of species, amazed that each was so intricately designed with a life and a beauty of its own. Celeste bought garden clothes, boots, and a pickup truck, and Charles accompanied her to the nursery to help with the hauling. Lean and limber, perfectly built for gardening, he learned to build a proper compost pile, prepare a fertile bed, apply the proper insecticides and fertilizers, dig a hole just deep enough, trim the trees at the right time, and lay out the plants and bushes in a pleasing way.

Celeste no longer received dozens of invitations, nor did many of her "friends" call to chat. Yet she discovered among the crowd of former sycophants and power seekers, a few sincere and wonderful friends. She thought to herself that this experience was somewhat like weeding an overgrown garden and nurturing a fresh one. She was left with friendships worth having, and she had made some new ones as well. Betsy called regularly and they sometimes lunched together in the Solarium, away from the gossipy glare of the Washington crowd. Sally was busy learning the ropes of her new job at the paper, but she sometimes joined them. She and Griff were now joined at the hip, and although Griff was very content with their relationship, he was less content at work.

Chapter 21

Griff had stayed on to work for the new chairman of the Senate Intelligence Committee, Charlie Wong, a left fringe, third term Democrat from the State of Oregon. Wong had been next in line for the chairmanship and although there was serious opposition to elevating him, powerful leftist supporters in the international community stepped up to the plate and got him in. Despite Amos's earnest and ongoing efforts to offer an outstretched hand of friendship across the seas, Wong maintained that the United States was a foreign policy bully and its undeniable antagonists were its victims. When Griff presented various reports on specific issues that belied this point of view, Wong would go off on an emotional harangue that could last for an hour or more and be clearly heard down the end of the long hall. Before he read it, he would scream in unmentionable terms that the outcome of the report was a predicate laid down before the report was written and that the authors had simply cherry-picked the inputs to achieve the result they wanted.

Wong blamed America for the Saudi-Iranian incident, shouting that we had destroyed their economies and hadn't done a damn thing to compensate for it. During his worst diatribes, he reverted to his ingrained propensity for hate speech, shouting at the top of his lungs that if only Israel would surrender its home on Arab land and resettle its Jews in Alaska or on a melting ice floe in the Arctic for all he cared, all of the problems of the Middle East would go away. At first Griff wrote memoranda spelling out the complicated history of Palestine and Israel in a meticulous and evenhanded way, careful to provide cogent arguments to separate the issues and celebrate the two-state solution, but Wong simply put these memos into the shredder. Now Griff just clamed up when Wong got into one of these fits but silence seemed to anger him even more.

Increasingly, Griff was frustrated by Wong's outbursts, by his refusal to read his papers, to give even modest credence to sworn testimony, to read academic papers that disagreed with his beliefs, or to review the unedited raw material that had been the basis of the analytical papers he had rejected. Contemptuous of colleagues who openly disagreed with his opinions, disdainful of those who opted for silence, Wong had no friends among them. The only things he unequivocably approved of were the pork and the bundlers that assured his re-election.

Griff's patience was already wearing thin when Wong went public with sensitive top-secret security matters, and he decided that he could no longer look the other way. He wrote a one-line letter of resignation, put his security badge on the desk, said goodbye to his colleagues, put his photographs and his diplomas into his otherwise empty briefcase and walked out of his office with a great sense of relief and a burning desire to take a hot shower.

Since Winn's death he had carried a heavy heart with him, especially in the places where he and Winn had shared so much camaraderie, so much common cause and so many intellectual exchanges. He hadn't realized how much he missed him until he closed his office door for the last time. It was like reaching the final page of a book of many parts, some pleasing, some exciting, some meaningful, and closing it with sadness that it was finished, that there was no more.

As he walked down the familiar corridors and left the building that he knew like the back of his hand, the place that was his daily destination for more than twenty years, Griff felt a twinge of anxiety, a gnawing fear of the great unknown.

Yet truth be told, the Senate had gone mad many years before. Most of its members were out of control, seemingly reigning over fiefdoms that were in reality lorded over by influential lobbyists and by the staffers who were in bed with them. The "noblesse oblige" breed of public servant had disappeared. Winn was the last of them. Now only the flotsam and jetsam remained, self-absorbed members who had forgotten that they were elected to serve the people and had ceded the power vested in them to those who would fill their campaign coffers.

Griff walked away, breathed fresh air and welcomed the warmth of the noonday sun as it brushed across his face. It felt good.

Chapter 22

Griff had held onto his apartment because he just hadn't gotten around to putting it on the market, but Sally's place was home. When he got there, he took off his shoes, poured a tall glass of strawberry Kool-aid, kicked back in his leather lounge chair and turned on the TV. For the first time in his life, he watched a magistrate preside over petty court claims and then a re-run of an old tennis match. Looking for an activity to fill more time Griff decided to surprise Sally with dinner, which he picked up at a popular eatery in Georgetown. He bought some nice flowers, the tropical kind Sally liked, and he set the table with care. He checked with Sally and when he figured she was almost home, he lit the dinner candles, looked over his handiwork, moved the flatware until each piece was exactly one inch from the edge of the table just as his mother had taught him, and he waited.

Sally strolled in, looked at the table, inhaled the fragrance of the flowers, opened the oven door to see what smelled so good, looked at Griff with a raised eyebrow, and said, "What's up?"

"What do you mean, what's up? Just because I wanted to surprise you with a nice dinner, something needs to be "up"?

"Yup," replied Sally. "I know you, Griff. Something is definitely up."

"Got me, there. I'll fill you in over dinner."

Griff told Sally all that had occurred that day, and she was not surprised that Griff had walked out. She was surprised that he had stayed so long. This Wong fellow was a nutcase.

"Have you thought about your next move?" Sally asked.

"Not really. I've been doing the same thing for a long time, and I'd like to take a timeout to explore other possibilities. I've got enough cash on hand to last for at least a year without touching my investments, and I'd like to see what's out there before I jump back into the fray."

"Sounds good to me." Sally's lips curled in that flirtatious way that always made him smile. "Just make sure you're not too rested when I get home. I still need a little sleep."

Chapter 23

President Amos Jackson had anticipated taking some heat for the roundup, but he hadn't expected it to be so virulent. The left-wing blogs were beating him over the head on a daily basis on the due process issues; the right-wing blogs were beating him over the head on a daily basis on the security breach issues; the print media were beating him over the head on a daily basis on anything they thought would improve circulation; the House and Senate members on both sides of the aisle were beating him over the head on any side of the issue that got them face time; and ambitious politicians with an eye to succession were beating him over the head in op-eds if only to get their names spelled right. Some days, Amos felt like the proverbial dartboard and on those days, even Amos had difficulty maintaining his sense of humor and his usually unruffled attitude toward the vicissitudes of public life.

In spite of the harsh distractions, Amos was working hard on the environmental initiative because he deeply believed it held real possibilities for a better world. With the soul of an idealist, tempered by realism and his pragmatic approach to getting things done, he believed that common purpose was the thread that would bind people and nations together. What better common purpose than a cleaner and safer planet?

Amos feared that the growing scarcity of clean water, especially in North Africa, the Middle East, and the Sub-Continent could lead to small but devastating wars over water resources; that the hazardous lack of clean air in industrial cities could cause sickness and rebellion, that unmet agricultural needs could cause widespread starvation, and that the continuing threat of major flooding in coastal regions could bring great loss of life. He wanted to tackle these problems in an aggressive way, but he knew he had to move cautiously so that he would not be marked as an environmental bully.

Although he had not yet settled on the best way to achieve his objectives, he was determined to make a genuine effort to bring India and China in as the prime movers and shakers in this endeavor, prodding them to take the lead. He believed if they were nudged to the forefront, they would welcome U.S. partnership in solving the environmental problems in their own lands and that such a relationship would have the spin-off effect of binding them closer to the Western powers. Amos reflected that a power bloc of this strength would help tame the troublemakers, especially those who respected power above all else.

He genuinely believed this, but he was being to a large extent thwarted by the brouhaha of the Saudi-Iranian mess, and there was little he could do except speed up the return of the offenders without appearing weak and let the rest of the episode play itself out. After he got that mess out of the way, he would flesh out the details and figure out ways to implement his ideas.

Only Betsy knew how troubled he was. He was restless at night, got out of bed and walked the corridors so he wouldn't waken her. Betsy, who was both intuitive and kind, played along because she knew he sometimes needed time and space to figure things out without worrying over her. But once in a while when he was gone for too long, she put on her robe and joined him in the corridor.

She said not a word, just fell into step beside him, and they walked together until he took her hand and led her back to bed. The power of their love was never stronger than at these times of silence and the pull of their attraction for one another was never more passionate.

For all the adoration and opportunities that came Amos's way, for all the women who were attracted to this powerful and gregarious man and let him know it, only Betsy captivated him. She was the love of his life.

Chapter 24

For almost forty years, lobbyists were ubiquitous on Capitol Hill. Now there were a mind-boggling 45,000 of them. Not just in the corridors and the member's offices as in days of yore, but everywhere. Former members, and there were hundreds of them, had Floor and Cloakroom access; foreign lobbyists and major contributors broke all the rules without fear of retribution; former staffers professing expertise, roamed freely, wrote legislation, rounded up votes like a party whip, openly glad-handed and entertained anyone who was willing to be courted, and no one interfered.

As one might expect in a jungle of this kind, there were multiple attempts to tame it. There were a plethora of judicial decisions and administrative rulebooks attempting to define the boundaries of the First Amendment's right to petition the government, but there were no willing enforcers. Through the years, the problem had grown like the green giant, but no one knew how to solve it nor did they really want to try. Every lobbyist could be found on one fundraising list or another, and these lists were the grease that kept the wheels turning. Lost among the high rollers were the public interest lobbyists who worked for little money and with limited success to represent the just grievances of the people.

The young Saudi Prince had become a fixture on the Hill, the Iranian representative, a newer face. Since the fiasco, they were glued together, an expedient partnership for sure. The Saudis wanted their Nighthawks with no strings attached. The Iranians wanted a five-year economic package with no strings attached and, with the heat turned on the President; they both wanted their emissaries returned with no admission of guilt and with apologies from the Americans for holding them.

Prince Nayif was trying to find out who on the committee was bottling up the Nighthawk sale, but in the sacred underground rule of personal privilege, no one was talking, not even the members he thought were in his pocket. Mahmoud Zandipour, the new Iranian attaché, was busy laying the groundwork for his job by introducing himself and making nice to everyone in his carefully prepared file of names and notations. He was also trying to strengthen his friendship with Nayif even though the ghosts of centuries past never ceased to linger in his thoughts.

"In Islam we have our differences, Nayif," said Mahmood, "but that which unites us in heaven is greater than that which divides us on earth. These Americans, they do not understand that our lives, yours and mine, are illuminated even brighter in death, and that we yearn for the day when we can join our martyred brothers. Inshallah. The Americans, they live in the present. They fear death while you and I, Nayif, we seek martyrdom when our souls can at last fly away to the Paradise that awaits us. We shall live forever. That is our power. While we sojourn on this earth we are patient, for centuries to us are but fleeting moments in time."

"Allah be praised, this is true," replied Nayif. "The President must have agreed to these Committee delays. We must take advantage of the pressure being applied to him by many and continue to apply pressure of our own. It is in our interest to damage him greatly for it is easier to shoot down a bird whose wings are broken. Perhaps in this way the others will see it is better to be our friend."

“Do you remember,” Mahmood chuckled, “the time when our countries had the Americans going in circles? They tried every carrot and stick they could think of. They were naive enough to believe we had turned our back on our nuclear ambitions, and now we have many nuclear warheads and the missiles to deliver them. It is true they have us in limbo with their missile shield, but we shall soon learn to penetrate it; then the clock for Israel’s destruction will begin ticking again; it is only a matter of time.”

“Do you remember, Nayif, when the Americans were blind enough to think you had removed the truth from your madrassa teachings? It is so are easy to lure them into wishful thinking. Even today your madrassas turn out jihadists who are waiting in long lines to be martyrs for Allah, young warriors who yearn to enter the Gates of Paradise. These Americans are a foolish people, and we shall spin them in circles again.”

“Inshallah.” replied Nayif. “We shall get our Nighthawks, and you shall get your package. Before this is over, diplomats the world over shall demand that the Americans apologize and return our embassy people to us. We are the best of peoples, and our embassy fools have shamed us. But they must be put to death as Allah wills it, not punished in the American way.”

“Allah hu Akbar.”

“Allah hu Akbar.”

“Ah,” said the Prince, “Here is the office of the committee chairman. I will introduce you to him. He thinks I am his good friend because I contribute much to his campaigns when he most needs the money. We shall ask for nothing today, only that he remember your name.”

Chapter 25

At Laurelwood the autumn leaves were strewn across the woodlands and lay in heaps of golden patches along the meandering meadows. The gentle slope that had once been bruised by the crush of burning metal had almost recovered, with only a trace of browned grass disclosing its earlier wounds.

Celeste and Charles were pleased with the outcome of their fall plantings and often strolled along the garden pathways to admire the fruits of their hard work. At dusk, they found a source of pleasure in watching rivers of birds fly in great waves across the soft grey sky. They sat on the patio with their bird book, eagerly learning the names of the migrating birds that were rushing south to seek a full belly and a warm perch. They learned which skyways carried northern water thrushes, lark sparrows, hooded warblers, and chestnut-collared longspurs, and they waited patiently to spot the songbirds that flew across the moon in the dark of night. Much of the time they sat in silence and as the days passed, their silence grew more comfortable and their need for each other grew stronger.

Although he was always in their thoughts, they never spoke of Winn. Both feared still that the mention of his name would somehow make his absence more painful, more permanent. Their hearts were too wounded, their grief too fresh to bring him back to life through memories. They needed time to heal. Though unspoken, this shared sorrow gave birth to a bond that comes only in such a way.

Fall melded into winter and the blankets of leaves turned into blankets of fluffy snow, the kind that was pretty to see and easy to clear. From time to time, Celeste still lunched with Betsy in the Solarium, and occasionally Betsy lunched and spent the afternoon at Laurelwood.

They found in each other traits that were so hard to find in those who were immersed first and foremost in the Washington world of politics where hidden agendas were the order of the day. In each other, they found trust and genuine friendship.

Sally joined their gab sessions whenever she could escape the strenuous demands of her new job. She had forged a close relationship with Betsy when she had done an in-depth series of feature stories on Betsy's early life, her days at Duke and her marriage to the President, and Griff had asked Sally to keep an eye on Celeste whenever she could spare the time. These three women with no children among them found common ground again and again and before long, they were sisters under the skin, a triumvirate never to be torn asunder. So rare in their unkind world of gossip and backbiting, of who's up and who's down, their friendship became a bulwark against the harsh scrutiny of a high profile political life. With each other, they could be real.

Betsy shared her concern that Amos was being so unfairly beaten up by his opponents and by the blogs and the media for doing what he had had to do to disrupt the Saudi-Iranian plot. Regardless, Amos, who loved his country with all his heart, was determined to see those treasonous public servants brought to justice without delay. Of course, Sally knew all that had transpired and she was appalled by the lopsided criticism. She would be careful to be fair but she recognized a lynching when she saw one, and she made a silent vow to try to right the ship.

Chapter 26

The "Gang of Ten," as they were called, was arraigned in the Federal District Courts for New York and the District of Columbia. They had been held in "protective custody" and at their arraignment, their team of lawyers agreed to consolidate the trial in the Federal District Court in D.C. The legal team requested that bond be set, but the Judge rejected this request.

After pre-trial motions, which included damning depositions and the disclosure of an overwhelming electronic trail of their guilt, the "Gang of Ten" pleaded "nolo contendre." In the end, they just wanted to get the best deal possible without dragging their families through the mud any longer.

Jake was gone, and Sally was on her own. She conferred with Feld, and they agreed that they would run a multi-media series not only covering the espionage story but also going into deep background to set the tone and present the facts without taint of political bias.

Sally reserved front-page space for the series. For editorial comment, she tapped the paper's veteran editorial page writer, widely respected as a straight shooter, and she personally lined up op-ed contributors who were well known for old-fashioned fairness and balance. She conferred with her headline editor, and asked that she collaborate with her on the story headlines. She also made it clear to the assignment editor that she wanted only seasoned reporters and video specialists, that all copy needed to be run by her well before deadline and the video output screened before it was posted. She did all of this in a low key and non-threatening way, stressing the spirit of teamwork and the pursuit of excellence. Everyone on the story met daily at 7:30 A.M. in the conference room to go over any glitches, update Sally on the day's assignments, and ask questions. Nothing was left to chance and everyone understood that Sally wanted to be directly involved. "If we do this right," Sally mused, "this story could be in the running for a Pulitzer."

With Sally's hands on the wheel, she made sure that Amos got a fair shake, that the Saudis and the Iranians got the scrutiny they deserved, that the "Gang of Ten" were not romanticized like the mafioso of the twenties, and that the newspaper, the Web, the nation and justice were well served.

The Washington Post series received plaudits from the critics. Even the blogs had good things to say. Sally had succeeded in changing the tone, in turning the finger towards the culprits instead of toward Amos, and the nasty criticism of him died down. The major dailies and other multimedia players followed suit, and soon Amos was a hero again.

The series won a Pulitzer, and Sally and Feld were a very happy pair. He had taken a gamble on her instincts, and they had both won.

"The Gang of Ten," having presented no defense to multiple charges of espionage, were sentenced to Federal prison for a total of 250 years. In Federal prison, the most civilized of American prisons, they would have a clean bed, a desk and chair, three nutritious meals a day, clean clothes, a daily shower, a minimum of 2 hours each day in the exercise yard, a job, time in the recreation room and library, and 2 family visits a month. Each would be eligible for parole after serving at least 15 years. As a result of their sorry misadventure, ten ordinary families were torn apart - nine men and one woman ripped from society and from their homes and their children because of their human frailties and their foolhardy hunger for gold.

The Saudi and the Iranians were returned to their countries in ignominious defeat, taken to Andrews Air Force base surrounded by an extravagant televised show of uniformed American military police. At Andrews, at Amos' direction, the Secretary of State and emissaries from Saudi Arabia and Iran held a joint press conference expressing their deep regret at the incident and their relief that the matter was satisfactorily resolved. They professed their high regard for one another and their determination to continue a close and mutually beneficial relationship. Amos hoped this facet of the espionage matter was closed and that there were no perilous loose ends lying around that would reopen it.

With the public pieces of the security breach mess behind him and with a cycle of domestic tranquility and economic prosperity giving him space to breathe, Amos turned his energies toward his global environmental initiative, which he fully intended would be the major achievement of his administration.

Chapter 27

Sally was exhausted from her efforts to get the espionage story right. She felt a little off kilter; thought she might be coming down with the flu, and just wanted to crawl into bed, pull the covers over her head, and sleep. Feld, proud of Sally's hard work in an almost fatherly way, told her to take a few days off and rest up. She hadn't had the time to groom a second in command, and he told not to worry, he'd cover for her and maybe Sophie would help out. He said it would feel good to get into the day-to-day fray again. Sally didn't object too much because she really felt lousy. She called Griff, and he seemed excited that she was coming home early.

Still at loose ends, Griff spent most of his time at home, much of it on the computer checking around for opportunities, keeping up with his investments, following the blogs and the on-line news coverage, and scrutinizing Sally's prowess with a professional and personal eye. For the first time in his adult life, he visited his parents once or twice a week and he took them to lunch in Georgetown, or they took him to lunch at the Congressional Country Club. They were delighted at his newfound interest in them, and he was surprised that he thoroughly enjoyed their company. On occasion they even cooked for him, trying out one of the simpler recipes they had learned in their cooking class adventure in the south of France. Griff was amused by the camaraderie they shared in the kitchen, just as amused by them as they seemed to be with each other.

After raised eyebrows at his previous relationships, Griff was relieved that they seemed genuinely fond of Sally. They said they found her bright and interesting and were relieved that he had found a "suitable" partner. His mother admired Sally's good taste in clothes, and his father admired her keen intellect and her status in the Washington hierarchy. He was especially awed that she seemed oblivious to the power she held at her fingertips and was impressed by the discretion with which she wielded it. A welcome addition to their dinner party "A" list, they were pleased that they could depend on her to see that Sophie assigned a good Style section reporter for their special evenings. In turn, Sally was amazed at their spunk and enthusiasm, by their wide-ranging interest in people and all things new and always tried to be at their parties and special occasions. This was all so new to Sally. Her circle of friends and family, people who really cared about her, was expanding and she liked it.

For the first few months of his life outside the pressure cooker Griff was content, but lately, with no fixed schedule of things to accomplish, no intellectual stimulation, he found himself thinking more and more about just one bottle of cold beer, one martini, or one stop at a Georgetown hangout where he could chat up the bartender. He pushed these thoughts away because he knew he had to. He was glad Sally was taking some time off. Maybe they could spend some time together just having fun.

Sally got home at about 2 o'clock, barely brushed Griff's cheek with a light touch of her lips, plopped across the sofa and fell fast asleep. Griff was disappointed but he waited patiently, watching her with the warmth and tenderness he felt whenever she was near. It had taken a long time to find this happiness, and he was going to do everything he could do to hold onto it. At 5 o'clock Griff whipped up some dinner, set the table and from time to time but to no avail, he made a little noise to get her up. Sally slept like a rock until 8 o'clock, stretched, groaned and tried to go back to sleep but Griff convinced her to join him for dinner. She sat at the dinner table, picked at the food on her plate but didn't eat most of it and went to bed.

Next morning, Griff heard Sally making awful sounds in the bathroom, guttural sounds - gagging, throwing up, and moaning. He helped her dress, put her in the car, and insisted they go to the Emergency Room at George Washington Hospital.

It was there that they learned that the pattern of their lives would change forever. This was so unexpected, so overwhelming, something they had never even thought about, never imagined. Sally was pregnant. She was 43 years old, a high-risk pregnancy by some standards, and Griff was 46, a bit old for a first time dad, but they were elated. There was no hesitation to their happiness, no second thoughts. Griff held on to Sally as if she might break, and Sally held on to Griff because he was now her protector; he would see to it that everything turned out all right.

They went home with lists of instructions, names of obstetricians, a projected due date, a prescription for pills to quiet the nausea, and feelings of joy at this mysterious work of creation. They sat on the sofa holding hands, Sally with her head on Griff's shoulder, Griff tilting his head to lean on hers, neither wanting to let go of the other, neither wanting to break the spell. Two hard driving and successful people with impressive resumes and a well ordered life suddenly realizing that the most important thing on earth was the little person growing inside of Sally's belly, a miracle that would change everything.

Chapter 28

When Abdullah al Amari arrived in Riyadh, the Kingdom's Royal Guards greeted him. They placed a blindfold on his eyes, a gag in his mouth, handcuffed him and placed him in the rear of a military vehicle. He was taken directly to a courtyard where the charges against him were read and the verdict was rendered. With agreement from the Saudi Royal family and the ulema, the esteemed council of religious leaders, and in strict accordance with sharia law, he was promptly beheaded. His head and his body were washed, wrapped in a white shroud and placed in a crude cardboard box for delivery to his family's house, which was on the outskirts of Riyadh in a place called Al Kharj. His family members received the box in silence for they feared for their own lives.

In keeping with religious tradition, he was buried the next day with only the males of his family permitted to attend the burial prayers. His mother and sisters had no choice but to remain at home to shed their tears and share their memories. None of them knew what Abdullah had done to so provoke the King's wrath that he would end Abdullah's life in such a dishonorable way. Nor did they dare to ask. They could only wail and lift their arms to Allah to plead mightily for the Intercession of the Prophets. If the Scales of Abdullah's good and evil deeds favored him, the Prophets could choose to save him from the fires of hell. The members of his family prayed hard for this was all they could do for him now.

Ahmed Tehrani and Hamid were flown to Tehran where a contingent of the Quds Force from the Revolutionary Guard Corps greeted them. They were immediately taken to the offices of President Farid Zahedi who personally spoke to them of his deep sadness that they had failed Allah and shamed Islam and for that reason, they had lost the keys to Paradise. This, Zahedi bellowed, had placed a heavy burden upon the Court to recommend the most just of punishments. The President informed Ahmed and Hamid that with the consent of the Grand Ayatollah, an agreement had been reached to propose to the Court a fitting punishment in accordance with sharia law. They now knew with certainty that their punishment was fixed and that it would be severe.

For nearly six months Ahmed and Hamid were fed insect infested gruel, which they choked down while squatting on the dirt floor of a damp, windowless and rat-ridden prison cell. In the oppressive heat of summer they were told the time had come for their punishment, and they were taken directly to the prison courtyard. The summer sunlight was painful to their eyes for their eyes had grown unaccustomed to light.

Ahmed and Hamid were blindfolded, led to a helicopter and flown a short distance to a place, they knew not where, and they were left there. The helicopter flew away, the last sound they would ever hear other than the pitiful howling of their own voices. They were trapped in the midst of an uninhabited and treacherous part of the Great Salt Desert, a place they had heard of only in scary childhood tales, an isolated place distinguished by a salt crust, quicksand marshes, intense sun, and dunes of sand and hopelessness. They prayed that death would come quickly, and it did. No word of their fate ever reached their families. They simply disappeared.

Chapter 29

When Feld heard Sally was pregnant he went into high gear. He sent Sarah shopping for a comfortable new sofa to replace the lumpy one in Sally's office, called in the maintenance crew and gave them a long list - repair the leaks in Sally's powder room, wash the carpet, replace the tiny refrigerator with a larger one, and wash the windows. He called a fancy Connecticut Avenue florist and personally ordered an expensive orchid plant for her desk. Sarah said she hadn't seen him beaming like this since she told him she was pregnant with Melanie. Secretly, Sarah began to collect crib blankets, stuffed animals, infant wear, and baby picture frames, all of which she tucked away in the far corner of her walk-in closet.

Celeste and Betsy were overjoyed by the news. Vicariously, this would be the pregnancy neither had ever experienced. They were fascinated with every detail, immersed in every aspect of Sally's progress. How much had she gained? What did the doctor say? Could they see the sonogram? How did she feel? What should she eat? How much did the baby weigh so far? Did she want to know if it was a boy or a girl? Had she thought of any names? Was she getting enough sleep? Could she keep up the pace at the office? Was there anything they could do to help? Two mother hens, and Sally didn't mind at all. Sally's mother was an infrequent voice on the phone, and the mothering they provided felt good.

Griff hovered. When they were together he treated her like a fragile china doll, and he watched her every move so that she wouldn't fall and break. It made her crazy. Lately he had begun to explore some serious job possibilities, and she was hoping one would pan out soon so he would get back to work and begin to focus on something other than on her. She knew he had had meetings over at the Pentagon, some at State, and one with a private intelligence-gathering firm. Because of the nature of his meetings and the character of her work, they discussed these meetings only in the broadest terms and avoided getting into the details.

The President knew about Griff's meetings at State because, unbeknownst to Griff, he had suggested them. The President was still kicking around in his mind some possibilities that would advance his environmental initiative and some of those possibilities involved spinning off an agency that was tethered to State and thus probably hindered from doing its best work. Amos was toying with the idea of making this agency independent, with powers of its own and a budget that couldn't be manhandled by the higher-ups.

Amos was increasingly convinced that the agency, the United States Agency for International Development, USAID, would have been a more efficient tool for economic development and humanitarian assistance in the war ravaged or disaster plagued nations in the Middle East, Africa and Southeast Asia, had it been able to operate outside of the constraints of the slow moving State Department, with the speed and agility of Defense, and without the bureaucratic and political conflicts inherent in the historic competition between these two behemoths. Too late to rewrite history, but if history was a measure, where effective development was concerned, poorly managed projects couldn't do it; over the top exhortations couldn't do it; untraceable cash couldn't do it; the dysfunctional UN couldn't do it; and the backlogged and bureaucratic World Bank couldn't do it. Amos thought that AID, as an independent agency, could be not only an effective economic development and humanitarian assistance agent but also an instrument for solving the severe environmental fallout of rapid and haphazard growth.

Amos, in keeping with his objectives, also envisioned that this independent agency could be the catalyst that would entice India and China to come to the table as equal partners. Since rapid development had exacerbated their own water and air problems and they needed technical assistance to cope with them, this aspect of AID's new role might have great appeal to them; and without their cooperation, meaningful opportunities for global cooperation on environmental issues would be difficult to achieve. He had thought long and hard on this issue, had received all sorts of issue papers and memoranda on it, perused AID's budget with a critical eye and was ready to make a decision.

To make it work, he needed someone he trusted, someone he liked, someone who had his fingers on the pulse of quickly changing world events, and someone with the intellect and the contacts that would enable him to connect the dots and move the initiative forward. The unfortunate events of this past year had given him a close look at such a man, and he was all set to talk to Griff.

With the return of the embassy attaches to their home countries, the espionage episode had disappeared from view, and as far as Amos knew there were no whispers of Griff's involvement, no hint of retribution.

Chapter 30

The first breath of springtime popped up in the bright yellow forsythia that bordered the south boundary of Laurelwood. Along its winding meadows, fields of early yellow daffodils danced gracefully to the gentle Maryland breezes, seemingly tipping their hats to this promising time of the year. It was the season Celeste loved the most, the season of colors that would paint the earth, of fragrances that would permeate the atmosphere; the time when birds that had flown south in late fall would return to their nests in the tall oaks, the delicate wild dogwoods, and the sturdy tulip poplars that peppered the grounds. It was the season of renewal and Celeste was nourished by the fresh life it brought with it. This spring was a particularly poignant time for her. It was time to put the estate on the market. She put off calling Roberta. She just couldn't bring herself to take that final step.

Early in June, Roberta called Celeste, and set up an appointment to discuss the listing. Roberta was amazed to see the outcome of her suggestions. The place was enchanting, greatly enhanced by the new plantings and the marvelous splashes of color, not only at the entrance but thoughtfully and artistically spread across the grounds. Celeste and Roberta sat at the breakfast room table and went over the papers, and when they were complete and ready for her signature, Celeste just fell apart. She couldn't do it. Roberta, who had been around the block more than once, sensed that something fundamental, had changed. She suggested to Celeste that she put aside any thought of selling the place for another year or so, until she had gotten her bearings and was sure it was something she wanted to do, and they parted as friends.

Charles was not surprised by Celeste's decision. Over the past months he had watched her emerge from her cocoon. He had seen first hand the changes that had come slowly in the beginning; but then, like the chrysalis just before it emerges into a butterfly, she began to spread her wings and test them to see if she could really fly. With great joy, Charles watched her come into her own. He watched her stand tall and eagerly feed on the promise of each new day. He had seen all of it and the love he had always felt for her, a love he had carefully concealed, a love that he believed inappropriate and hopeless, this love was now unleashed in his every thought; but he still held fast to the restraint that was second nature to him now.

Ever since she decided to stay, Celeste felt a great sense of relief. She took long solitary walks through the garden pathways admiring the results of her toil and thinking through the events of the recent past. She believed that she couldn't have survived without Charles and felt his presence keenly even when he was nowhere about. Charles watched from afar, and he was content just knowing that she had found a measure of contentment. When she returned to the house in late afternoon he would greet her with a ready smile and a very dry martini, which was her favorite afternoon cocktail. After a time Celeste refused to drink alone and insisted that Charles join her. He resisted at first but slipped into joining her more easily than he had thought possible, and at long last he felt comfortable enough to call her Celeste.

Sally's pregnancy brought a new interest into Celeste's life. With help from a knitting shop in Bethesda, she began knitting little baby things. On one of her knitting treks she saw an antique cradle in the window of a shop nearby, and in an impetuous moment she went inside and bought it. Somewhat embarrassed, she set it near the fireplace in the breakfast room and told Charles she thought it would be a convenience in case Sally brought the baby by. She also bought wool and a beautiful but intricate pattern for a crib Afghan and conscientiously began to crochet it. Still, once in a while she hit a tricky spot and when she did, she and Charles sat side by side, Charles trying to interpret the pattern for her and Celeste working hard to follow his patient instructions.

Celeste now dressed more casually than before, mostly in jeans and t-shirts during the day and in nice slacks and a silk shirt for evenings. Even on dressy occasions she no longer bothered to use much makeup and dispensed altogether with perfume and high heels. Although she still accepted an occasional invitation for an evening out, more and more she was happiest spending time at home with Charles. They played competitive games of Scrabble and Trivia, read a good book, listened to good music, watched some TV but not much, and memory-by-memory they shared their childhood stories and spoke of their values. Some of the time they just sat quietly and there was no discomfort in their silences.

Now Celeste could roam through the rooms without feelings of unease, without replaying the old and ugly memories. Now she could dwell on the newness of her life in this place, and she felt in harmony with it. Happy with the improvements she and Charles had made to the grounds, she decided to do the same to the house.

Celeste discussed this decision with Charles, and they collaborated to find a Bethesda interior designer who was known to work cooperatively with his clients, which was important to Celeste. She wanted to change this house to express her own tastes and erase the remnants of her parent's lives, stale leftovers of the early years she was trying to forget.

Chapter 31

After a series of conversations with an undersecretary and then with the Secretary of State, Griff was scheduled to meet with the President. Molly Bentsen and the President's chief of staff were already in the oval office when Griff was escorted in. Amos congratulated him on the news about Sally's pregnancy, made some small talk and feeling more than a bit awkward, asked if they were planning to be married, and if they were, Betsy had suggested they marry in the White House. Griff was taken aback because he really hadn't thought about it. It simply hadn't entered his mind.

With a quizzical smile as if a light bulb had suddenly gone off in his head, he said, "Can I get back to you on that, sir?" Amos chuckled, and replied; "I haven't seen Betsy so excited about anything since my inauguration. It's kinda nice."

"Now for the business at hand Griff. I'm sure you've been well briefed on my intention to spin off AID from State. I can do this with an executive order, make it quick, avoid the obstacle course of the nominating process and steer clear of the squabbles and polemical arguments of a dysfunctional Congress. The Secretaries are on board with this and so are the key congressional leaders on both sides of the aisle. When you wash away the politics, they all realize we have to improve our environment to the extent that we can, and we have to encourage smart and orderly growth, especially in the developing nations where a lot of the growth is helter-skelter. There is a helluva lot we are doing already, but it will take at least a couple more lifetimes to get it right. Griff, with a concerted effort, I think you and I can achieve enough progress to make us glad that we took up the challenge."

"We have some measurable metrics to point to even now. So far, with international cooperation, we've voluntarily reduced carbon emissions worldwide much more in the last fifteen years than we ever thought we could. We've begun aggressive reforestation programs in Africa, South America and Southeast Asia that are producing green jobs and will eventually restore the rainforests. With worldwide support, we've begun to create no-build zones in coastal danger spots around the globe. We've worked closely with the scientific community to advance systemic ways to predict natural disasters that have already averted some calamities but much more work needs to be done before we can be confident that alarm bells will ring often enough and soon enough to sound useful warnings. With cooperation from willing participants, we've transcended a few national boundaries in desalination, river restoration and sustainable agriculture, enough to show that cooperation works but not enough to cure the problem."

"Here's the nub. I believe that to continue making progress, it is essential to strengthen our ties to China and India where environmental progress is tenuous at best. I worry that their dangerous environmental problems could cause serious unrest, but we can't begin to help them address the problem without their invitation, and they can't effectively address the problem without our technical support. Study after study show that the people in China need to breathe cleaner air and the people in India need to drink cleaner water. You know from your briefings that I believe we have to convince them to welcome our involvement if they are to achieve progress in these areas. Now that we are on a level playing field with India and China in economic clout, there's nothing we can't accomplish as a team. Once we've built up our personal relationships on these environmental issues, we can work together cooperatively on a whole host of other important issues."

"Griff, you have all the low-key leadership attributes I'm looking for in someone to spearhead this effort. It won't be easy. We've just got broad-brush strokes for now, and you will need to develop the programs and projects to make it all work. You've had time to recharge, Griff, and I know you can do it. Well, what do you say, friend?"

"That's quite a lot you've thrown at me, Mr. President, but the briefings prepared me to hear it. It's huge, sir. I've given it a great deal of thought, and I'm willing to give it a try if you think I'm right for the job. I can assure you, sir, that I would give it it all I've got."

"I have confidence in you, Griff. You've made no enemies in twenty years in a tough job and that says a lot. Molly will give you all the support you need over here. She will keep the overlapping departments and agencies in the loop, and she will be your day-to-day contact person, but my door will be open to you. If you need me Molly will set it up, but if she's not available, you can get through to me directly. This is very important to me, Griff."

The President stood, as did the others. He came around the desk, shook Griff's hand, put his arm around his shoulder, and said, "Get back to me on that personal matter, will you?" Both of them chuckled.

Chapter 32

Prince Nayif was summoned home. His Royal Highness, King Khalid wished to meet with him immediately upon his return. The Prince, the oldest son of Crown Prince Sabir, the King's younger brother, was taken from the airport in Jeddah to the King's favorite palace, which was on the shores of the Red Sea. From the moment he crossed the threshold of the arched granite entry and was led through the arcade that continued a long way beneath an upswept overhang, Prince Nayif felt great disquiet. For all the modernity of this sculpted white stone palace, the ancient laws still applied even to the privileged such as he. He prayed to Allah he had done nothing to displease the King.

The King was waiting for him in the Inner Courtyard. Through the Courtyard arches one could gaze at the sea, and because there was water surrounding the palace on every side, it appeared to be set on a secluded island, cut-off from escape.

Nayif's heart fluttered in fear. He dared not speak first but waited for the King to address him. "How was your journey, Nayif? Was it an easy one?"

Nervously making small talk, Nayif replied that it was, but it was long. The King motioned to those who attended him to offer fruit and drink to the traveler, and he too partook of the nourishment.

"Tell me of the progress we make on the Nighthawk sale, Nayif. It is of great interest to me."

Nayif tried to explain the delay caused by the rule of "personal privilege" but the King shook his head in dismay and stopped Nayif's in his tracks. "I shall provide greater resources for you. You must use them wisely and with speed so you can produce the result I seek. Your first duty is to get the Bill out of Committee and to the Floor where we have considerable persuasive powers to get it passed. There are several photogenic Senators who I am quite certain will lead the Floor effort. They will do this to save their own foolish necks. When the time is right I will give you personal files on each of them that will assure our success. We shall speak of this again in one month."

"How do you fare with our Persian brothers, Nayif? So long as we are stronger together than apart, we shall continue this partnership. If we are hindered by it, and you must keep me informed on this, then we shall each go our own way." Nayif nodded in agreement.

"I have an important task for you to perform upon your return to America. I have a gift for someone who is a valuable friend to the Kingdom. It is an expensive gift and you must guard it with great care. You must visit your father now, and he will tell you how to find her. You are to deliver it to her without mentioning the Giver. She will know." The King motioned for a box in which sat a huge emerald cut diamond ring, too large for an ordinary finger but not too large for a greedy one.

"Peace be upon you," said the King as he waved his hand in a sign of dismissal.

"Allah hu Akbar."

"Allah hu Akbar."

Waves of relief washed over Prince Nayif, for he knew that he had escaped serious censure for now. He would have to try harder to get the Nighthawk sale out of Committee. Inshallah.

Chapter 33

On a lovely September day, measure and notebook in hand, Bethesda interior designer Kenneth came to Laurelwood. Accompanied by Celeste, he spent the better part of an afternoon strolling through every one of its rooms. It was his way of getting a feel for a place, to have it speak to him as he sketched the rooms, took measurements, and jotted down ideas.

This visit also helped him get to know Celeste. He recorded her comments, observed her reactions to a few of his suggestions, and learned her favorite colors, her preferences, and the overall tone she wanted to achieve in the refurbishing of this very formal setting. He was pleased to learn that she was leaning toward a transformation to informality, comfort, and a soft neutral palette, accented by the antique Persian rugs she wanted to keep and by the contemporary art that she had recently begun collecting. This was the kind of challenge that appealed to him. He could see that she had excellent taste, and he felt he could pull together a design scheme that would feel right in this traditional setting and at the same time meet her expectations for a new look.

They left the kitchen for last. Charles was waiting for them there and offered tasty refreshments and polite conversation. Celeste introduced him as her friend, and although Kenneth wondered exactly what that meant, he could soon see that there was a close bond between them. He wondered if he would also need to please Charles who seemed to be a very nice man, but he decided to approach the matter with discretion and play it by ear for now.

After Kenneth left, Celeste took Charles on a grand tour of the rooms, explaining what she and Kenneth had discussed, passing on her own thoughts and asking Charles for his. Charles had opinions but he was too reticent to give them. This house belonged to Celeste and no matter how close they had become, he would never step beyond the bounds of propriety.

When they reached Celeste's bedroom suite, a place he had entered thousands of times, a place where he had brought Celeste juice and toast when she was under the weather, where he had opened the draperies to awaken her for an early engagement, where he had come to tell her that the guests had arrived, he felt something new in Celeste that made him pull back. Sensing his sudden reluctance, Celeste took him by the hand and guided him through the door. She had known for a while that this friendship would remain platonic unless she made the first move to change it, and she was determined to try. She wanted her world to be a world with Charles in it because her world without Charles was too incomplete to contemplate and her world with Charles was beautiful and whole. She had never loved before. She had been too wounded, too frightened to open her heart. She believed that Charles loved her, but she didn't know if he had acknowledged this even to himself. There was so much at stake; she had to take the risk.

"Come, Charles."

"Celeste, are you sure?"

"Charles, I have never been more sure of anything in my life."

They entered the room together, but it was Celeste who led Charles to the chaise, she who turned his face towards hers, she who first found his lips and tasted them, she who slowly unbuttoned his shirt and more quickly, her own, she who led him to the bed, and then in an instant, the flame that had seethed for so long beneath the surface of each of them, ignited in a blaze so hot that they lost all reason. Each and every restraint they had harbored simply vanished in that all-consuming fire. When the embers faded they stroked one another with tenderness, both of them euphoric that their daydreams had come to life, that the reality was more amazing than they had imagined, more perfect than they could have hoped for, and they vowed that they would guard this love, grow with it and believe in it.

It took time for Charles to shed the skins of subservience, to grow to full size as Celeste's equal partner, to stand shoulder to shoulder with those he might have served in the past, but thankfully he never shed the wisdom and the kindness that endeared him to anyone who got to know him well.

Celeste could now forgive those who had wronged her. She could forgive her father; she could forgive Winn, and most of all, she could forgive herself. Somewhere she had read that love is the prism through which we can learn to forgive, that love opens doors and closes circles. Now she knew that this was true.

Chapter 34

Griff had a full plate. The spin-off of AID from the State Department was smooth. Amos had eased the way with personal phone calls to the key players and with the appointment of the current director to the job of Deputy Secretary of State for Consular Affairs. He assigned Justice the job of perusing the State Department handbook to make sure the executive order to split off AID would stick, and he had Molly develop a new job description for Griff that was crafted to provide wide latitude. He made it clear to Griff that he wanted the agency design to avoid the bureaucratic trivia that cluttered State, and that he wanted to give him a free hand to design programs along with the power to implement them. On the other hand, Griff realized that to over-personalize the agency could invite problems when he was gone, and he intended to provide clarity to the job description after the mission had fully evolved.

First Griff knew he needed a competent and responsive staff. No way he could handle this huge assignment without one. He had to bring in knowledgeable personal staff and he had to do it in a way that would seamlessly blend them with the agency holdovers. He understood that it was essential to develop a master plan for AID's overall mission that clearly defined the goals and objectives of its new assignment, and he had to prioritize them in a way that would provide early success. He also needed a two year plan with specific projects and target dates, a line item budget that would cover the first two years of operation, line item projections for the next two years, and ballpark projections for the out years.

As for himself, he had to figure out the contacts he needed to make and the order in which he needed to make them, and he needed to do all of this without ruffling too many feathers over at State or in some instances, at Defense. Above all he needed to keep Molly in the loop all the way so she could effectively perform her job as chief integrator among the departments, agencies, key White House personnel, and the President.

In so many ways his twenty years on the Hill had prepared him well for this job. He had already learned to look over his left shoulder for the inevitable stumbling blocks, look over his right shoulder for the little people who thrived on the game of tripping up the real players, and at the same time, look straight ahead toward the goal posts. This was a big job and although Griff felt invigorated by its challenges, he was realistic about the difficulties that were inherent in such a massive undertaking.

He also had Sally to think about. His calendar now included daddy and mommy classes. At first he thought they were just silly, but after a while he began to enjoy the camaraderie of the others who were going through the same experience. As Sally's belly grew the charismatic instructor got them to talk to the baby, to feel its movements, to discuss their expectations of labor and delivery and to give voice to their fears. All of this was so far removed from the high-powered days he and Sally were living, they sometimes wondered if they were really suited for parenthood, if they would ever get the hang of it. It helped that the other first-timers in the class felt these same pangs of insecurity, and it helped to chat with them.

With so much going on, Griff still hadn't mentioned Amos' suggestion that they marry. To Griff it would make no difference in their relationship, just a piece of paper to tuck away in the safe deposit box along with their other legal papers. Where Sally was concerned, Griff was afraid that after two hideous marriages she would recoil at the thought, and he didn't want to chance such a reaction. He didn't know if he could handle it. So he put aside any mention for now.

Sally's life at the office was also challenging but in a very different way. Though the days were demanding she had slipped without great difficulty into her job as managing editor. Now Feld helped her out more than he had first planned because he was very protective of her general well being. Three mornings a week, he brought in an insulated bag with nourishing food inside and emptied its contents into the refrigerator. There were post-it notes on the plastic containers that said the chicken soup with matzoh balls was to be heated on level 5 for 3 minutes, the stuffed chicken breast on level 3 for 1 ½ minutes, the vegetables on level 4 for 2 minutes, the tuna salad to be eaten by Thursday, and the egg salad by Friday, as well as an assortment of yogurt, and cartons of skim milk. Each week he also brought in a sliced challah and a basket of fruit – tangerines, apples, bananas and grapes with a note attached that said, "at least two servings each day." If Sally had eaten everything Sarah sent in, she would have gained at least twice the weight of the doctor's strict limits. She ate less than half and shared the other half with Sophie, who was now her assistant managing editor, her right arm, and her co-conspirator in scarfing up Sarah's food for Feld's weekly inspection.

It seemed as though everyone around Sally was as committed to this baby as they were protective of her, and on some days, especially the days when the baby was active and Sally's schedule was full, she was grateful for the support. Before her pregnancy she would have rebelled against such coddling. It would have felt overbearing and childish. But these days, with inexpicable emotions bubbling up at the strangest times, she didn't mind a little pampering.

Once in a while Sally even felt the urge to phone her mother but their relationship was cemented in a routine that didn't encourage spur of the moment contact, and Sally thought it would be too awkward to change it now. She buried the urge but the thought never completely went away.

Chapter 35

Prince Nayif knew that he was under the gun. He had to make headway on the Nighthawk sale, and he needed some new ideas on how to break the deadlock. With more money to spread around he would see if some of his contacts would weaken and help him out.

In the meantime he would deliver the gift and perhaps get a point or two for that. He called the number he was given and was told to come the next day precisely at 9 o'clock in the morning. Following the instructions his father had written for him, he drove to Potomac, turned up River Road two lanes beyond Fox Meadow, turned left at an unidentified lane, drove to the end of it, and parked at the entry of a huge mansion just as he had been told to do.

It was an imposing white house. There were triple Roman columns with curled designs at the top supporting the spacious portico and antique Foo Dogs sitting on either side of its twelve-foot heavily paneled black entry doors. Enormous round brass doorknobs were centered on each door that needed two hands for turning. Nayif pressed the speaker button. He was asked his name and the door was immediately opened.

An olive skinned gentleman in a dark blue blazer with an open throated striped shirt greeted him and asked him to follow. He was led through a huge entry hall that continued beneath a suspended double staircase into the library, and he was told to wait there. As he walked through the hall he took in the very formal living room on the left, decorated with Aubusson rugs, French impressionist paintings, and ornate Louis XV furnishings, but strangely, on his right, where one would expect openings to other rooms, there were none. There was only a solid wall ornamented with moldings and paintings.

The library was a handsome room, heavily masculine in its décor. The walls were of rich mahogany, and the bookshelves were filled with leather bound books displaying gold embossed titles. A striking camel, black and ivory antique Persian hunting rug covered the wide plank hardwood floors. Sitting on the rug opposite each other, were huge tufted black leather tuxedo styled sofas with wide rolled arms, one of them boasting a leopard skin with head and teeth intact draped casually over its back. On either side of the black marble fireplace surrounds were tall winged gargoyles that led the eye to a gilt framed mirror that rested on the mantle and reached almost to ceiling height. The ceiling was covered in a mural of voluptuous winged maidens with angelic faces scattered across a background of sky with clouds so deftly painted that they seemed to move. Even Nayif, who was quite accustomed to lavish surroundings, was impressed.

In about fifteen minutes the gentleman reappeared and motioned for him to follow. They walked past the floating staircase and entered a dark passageway that seemed to go into another building behind the house, then came to a dimly lit hall that led to a narrow staircase. The gentleman led him up the staircase to a door just opposite it. He opened the door and asked Nayif to wait again.

The room had a definite Asian flair – soft creams and golds, a six panel incised Asian floor screen, a Chinese rug, and a low seating arrangement. In came a beautiful Asian looking woman in a pencil slim dress of gold damask with a huge round diamond dangling from an almost invisible gold neck chain. She nodded to Nayif, and said, "I am told that you have a package for me from the Giver. It is late in coming but I am pleased that it has arrived. You must convey my gratitude and you must tell the Giver that I am honored to be of service."

Prince Nayif handed the small package to the lady. She did not open it in his presence. The gentleman who had been waiting just outside the door escorted him to his car. Nayif realized there had been no names mentioned other than his own.

Chapter 36

Griff's job was exhilarating. He had been away from the pressure cooker for so long that he had forgotten the adrenalin rush that comes with creativity and accomplishment. He succeeded in pulling together a pretty good staff of planners, environmentalists, project managers and administrators. They were people he knew and respected, and he made it clear to them that they were expected to function as team players. He informed the veteran staffers as well that a condition of their continued employment was unambiguous acceptance of the new mission along with a genuine commitment to the teamwork concept. Transfers to State or to the Pentagon or early retirements were offered to those who displayed a pattern of obstructionist behavior. Griff chuckled to himself that over at State or at the Pentagon, obstructionist behavior was the order of the day and wouldn't even be noticed.

The teamwork approach was promoted through senior staff meetings that were a blend of holdover staffers sitting side by side with new people. Blended teams of planners were formed to produce the master plan, the two-year plan and the budget; teams of project managers and environmentalists were formed to flesh out the priorities; legislative teams were formed to take care of the congressional committees; and a public information team was set up to handle the public inquiries and the press.

Griff encouraged a culture of optimism and cooperation, an open exchange of ideas, systematic coordination and communication, and all the while he continued to weed out the surviving saboteurs and lone rangers. With intelligent leadership and a steady hand at the wheel, it wasn't long before Griff had a cohesive staff he could depend on.

Now he felt he could get out of the office and meet more of the people who could help him execute the plan. He set up a lunch with Raj Singh, the old college friend who had joined up with him during his trek to India. They had spent a few days together in Calcutta and had traveled to Nepal with the intention of joining a Himalayan climb, but Raj had picked up a bad case of dysentery in Calcutta and Griff hadn't felt right leaving him behind. They hung out at a base camp until Raj was strong enough to travel and then cut the trip short and came home. Griff wanted to touch base with him and ask if he could use him as a sounding board.

Raj, a brilliant academic, was teaching economics at Georgetown, and though Griff kept up with him now and then, he hadn't seen him for quite a while. Raj had come to the Rotunda to sign the guest book for Winn's send-off, and Griff thanked him for that. He brought Raj up to date on Sally and the baby they were expecting, but he found it too painful to speak at length of Winn, and Raj understood.

He had read about Griff's new job and congratulated him. He wholeheartedly approved of the spin-off and expanded mission of AID and of Griff's good sense in settling down with Sally. "Whatever you do when the baby comes, I'd like to be there. As far as using me as a sounding board, I've got some down time right now and I can't think of anything I'd rather do. India is so diverse, such a mix of cultures, shaped by so many different influences, I can help you sort it through."

"They've made some progress in Calcutta since our trip. They've got an upgraded subway system and they've made first-rate improvements to my favorite bookstores. The wealthy classes continue to lead sophisticated lives with their big houses, their servants, their cultural pursuits, but for the most part Calcutta remains a hellhole. It's still a place that's rampant with typhoid, with teeming slums where the sewage and the rats run together through the alleys unchecked. Even the bottled water is suspect. Have you been briefing India's lobbyists?"

"Which ones? They have got a slew of them, different ones for different issues and different places; one for Mumbai, one for Dehli, one for Calcutta, one for the Bengalis, one for the Kashmiris, one for rural areas, one for electrification, one for medicine, and on and on. Raj chuckled, "That's India. Lots of problems! Lots of voices! You've got your work cut out for you."

Griff replied, "AID has been feeding them a big chunk of change already. I've assured the lobbyists that the bottom line is not going to change except to their advantage but it may be redirected. Did the same for the lobbyists for China."

"China is complex, Griff. More complex than India, if that's possible! If you like, I can set up a lunch date to introduce you to Jimmy Wu. He chairs the department of Chinese history at the University, understands the complexities better than anyone I know, and he's very keyed into the current players."

"I'd like that very much." Raj sent Jimmy a text message, got an instant reply, and the meeting was set up at the University for the next day.

Raj and Jimmy developed a real passion for Griff's mission. With their enthusiastic assistance, a Global Environmental Initiative Conference, with financial, technical, planning and administrative support from AID, was set up under the aegis of Georgetown University's School of International Studies, and prominent department chairmen and faculty from the University joined with AID to invite the conferees.

President Jackson gave the major address at the plenary session of the first conference, and high-placed luminaries from China and India followed on day two and day three. The president of the University who was a well-respected figure on the international scene introduced all of the luncheon speakers. India and China agreed to send distinguished specialists to the planning sessions for the next conference, which was well attended by most of the major countries, regional bodies, and technical experts from around the world. They were happy to meet with one another in a substantive forum rather than pretend they were doing business at the UN.

It was more than Griff could ever have hoped for. With the prestigious University's continued involvement, the Conference became a permanent forum that brought the principal players together. The relationships that developed through the Conference and especially through its permanent committees, served as a major catalyst to move the President's agenda forward.

From the first Amos was more than satisfied that his instincts on Griff had been on target, and Griff was satisfied with the extraordinary opportunities offered by the partnership of AID with the Global Environmental Initiative Conference. His job was challenging. His personal life was great. His recovery was enduring. What more could a guy want?

Chapter 37

His Royal Highness, King Khalid, and the Iranian President Farid Zahedi were not too happy with Nayif or Mahmood. Neither of them had produced the goods. The Saudi Nighthawk sale appeared to be off the table, and the Iranian economic package had been transferred to AID's budget where it was rumored for re-negotiation. Mahmood had reported that there would be more strings, troubling strings that would include fail-safe financial checks and balances to safeguard against the continued channeling of Iranian funds to terrorist groups.

King Khalid and President Zahedi agreed to meet again, this time in the Islamic Republic of Iran. With a lack of self-awareness Khalid chuckled to himself that this so-called democracy was so caught up in its never-ending attempts to snooker the West that it was going to be unwittingly snookered into caving to the West's conditions for an economic bailout. The King scoffed that this bogus democracy was merely a hodgepodge government of factions and personalities with no one capable of making big decisions. In his own country he could still make things happen with a flick of the wrist. But for now he needed Iran as an ally so he had agreed to come to Zahedi. Next time he would insist that Zahedi come to him.

The meeting was set up in Zahedi's residence in the ultra modern northern sector of Tehran. An Iranian made limousine carried the King through an orderly network of streets, which were busy with traffic and people. Through dark tinted windows the King saw women walking on the sidewalks and in the parks in Western dress with no covering on their heads. He was enraged that there were no "modesty police" on the streets to arrest them. The dark-eyed raven-haired Iranian women were so beautiful that he lowered his head so that he could not see them and with great fervor, he prayed "May Allah keep me on the path to Paradise. May the Prophet guide me in the way of righteousness! May I hold only pure thoughts! Allah hu Akbar." At last the limousine arrived at the residence where there were no shameless women flaunting their hair, and he sighed with relief.

Zahedi greeted His Royal Highness with respect and they retired to the meeting room, a palatial room with Louis XV furnishings, exquisite Persian carpets and azure and white mosaics on the walls. The King settled into a blue silk settee softened with azure and gold downy cushions, and he began the conversation.

"My nephew is a buffoon who hides behind his father's riches and his mother's abaya. His brain is so small that I have to do his thinking for him. Perhaps with an easier plan he can move the Great Satan to the finish, but I can assure you I will not be patient much longer."

"Mahmood is no better," said Zahedi. "I have a replacement waiting in the wings. But let us see if we can squeeze dry these two bumblers before I recall him. I have a plan. You know this Griffin Foster?"

"Of course! He was Ainsley's, how you say in America, his alter ego? He was the loose end but after Ainsley's misfortune, he disappeared before we could tie it. Our contact did not find him again until it was too late. He was our undoing. When the time is right we will finish the job, but now he may be of use to us. Tell me of the new plan."

"Your Royal Highness, our first plan was too difficult. It needed too many stones to kill too many birds. This plan is simple. We kill many birds with one stone. Our loose end is now a big man. He holds many strings. He holds our purse strings and if he desired, he could spring your Nighthawks. He is close to the foolish American President who demeans us as if we are children. He does not understand that we are the best of peoples. The President's wife has befriended Foster's woman who is now heavy with child. With no shame, Foster and his woman live in sin and we both know that sharia law deems it a moral obligation to punish these fornicators. This plan shall make the American infidels tremble. They shall go down on their knees before us. Your Nighthawks and my economic package will be a small price to pay."

"Inshallah"

"Allah hu Akbar"

"Allah hu Akbar"

"Ah," exclaimed the King. "The Prophet, blessed be He, has set us apart with wisdom beyond all others, and I begin to see where you are going. Tell me more of this."

Chapter 38

Prince Nayif was making no headway. He was being pressured by his embassy for a report on the Nighthawks, but he was putting it off because he had nothing to report. He was tired of sweating it out and decided to change his tactics.

Until now he had avoided meeting with Kathy Asher, the powerful Counselor to the Senate Committee on Foreign Relations. She was shapely and when he looked at her, embarrassing things happened to him. He would just have to calm down and talk to her.

For many years Nayif was promised to Aiaisha, a girl he had not yet met. The arrangement was made twelve years before, when he was fifteen and she was only five. On his last visit home his father told him they would make final plans for the wedding when his tour of duty was finished. More and more his reaction to young women shamed him even in his sleep, and he prayed that marriage would cure his affliction.

Kathy Asher, who was known not only for her wide-ranging knowledge of foreign policy but also for her tiny waist, huge breasts, and a big brain to match, had noticed Prince Nayif glancing at her out of the corner of his eye. Accustomed as she was to the ogling stares of men, she was amused by his obvious reluctance to approach her. She knew a repressed man when she saw one, and she had no doubt that his behavior had more than a little to do with his birthplace. He would be a challenge and she liked challenges, especially this kind.

The day before his appointment with Miss Asher, he could think of nothing else. Without warning, his thoughts brought on his affliction and in the blink of an eye, he was shamed. For his appointment he decided to bring a large umbrella in case he needed to hide this affliction.

Then he knelt on his prayer rug and asked Allah to forgive him for his sins, but he did not resolve that he would not repeat them.

Nayif appeared in Kathy's office on the fourth floor of the Dirksen Office Building promptly at 2 o'clock in the afternoon. He was asked to wait in the reception area, and he took this opportunity to compose himself with deep breaths and silent recitations of the Koran. He was convinced that his mission was a noble one for his country was the best of countries, and Allah, the all-powerful, blessed be He, would help him win in the end. But, there was a fear in him that he could not shake because he believed that the King would not tolerate failure and that his punishment would be grave.

At 3 o'clock, Kathy came out of her office to greet Nayif. He could not help observing that she was dressed in black high-heeled sandals with ruby-red painted toenails and a belted grey flannel pantsuit buttoned only to a place where her breasts came together. He stood swiftly and they shook hands. She apologized for the delay but explained she had been trying to get an update on the Nighthawk sale and was having some difficulty getting anything definitive. "Can you find something to do on the Hill until about five? Call me on my private line, and we'll go from there." She handed him a card with her private number scribbled on it.

Promptly at five, Nayif called and was told Kathy was still working on his issue. Could he meet her at six at the First Street entrance, and they'd go from there.

Nayif was there on time and was relieved that Kathy was waiting for him. She said she needed a strong cup of coffee and suggested they go across to the Russell Office Building coffee shop where they could relax and go over his problem unhurriedly. Nayif was eager to get this information but he was also nervous to sit alone with a woman in a social setting, especially this woman. When they got there, Kathy shed her jacket, and though Nayif knew he needed to concentrate on her words, he could only concentrate on the tight scoop-neck shirt that clung to her voluptuous breasts. Kathy said, "Prince Nayif, I am still digging around but no one is giving me anything I can put my teeth into. I'm still not sure whether this sale is on or off, but I want you to know that I understand how important this deal is to the Kingdom, and I will keep trying to flesh out the details."

"This is indeed a vital issue for the Kingdom, and I know you hold many keys to unlock many doors. If you are on the issue I believe I will learn what has become of the sale. Your people hunger for this deal also. It would mean many jobs, and how do you say, a shot in the arm for Boeing, no?"

"Let me bring you up to date on what I've discovered so far. May I call you Nayif?" He nodded. "I skipped lunch today. Just didn't have the time and I am absolutely famished. I live just a short walk away, and there are some really good leftovers in my frig. I'll fill you in over dinner. Okay?"

What could he do? He had to get as much information as he could on the sale. He nodded again.

Kathy's apartment was sparsely furnished with modern lounge chairs and a leather sofa in a soft neutral tone. The room was accented with matching Plexiglas occasional tables, matching lamps and two huge abstract paintings, one over the fireplace and the other in the entry hall. There was no bric-a-brac, no clutter, nothing personal. Obviously, domesticity was not Kathy's strong suit.

A couple of placemats on the cocktail table, a few cartons of re-heated Japanese carryout, a bowl of fresh fruit, a bottle of saki, and dinner was served. It was forbidden for Nayif to sit at a table where alcohol was present, but this was an important meeting, and he prayed that Allah would forgive him.

Kathy excused herself and said she was going to change into something comfortable. She returned in a white terry robe loosely tied at the waist. She sat on the sofa next to Nayif and told him to help himself to the food, and after he had filled his plate, she leaned over to fill hers. Her breast brushed his arm, and he felt heat on his face and fire in his groin. She sat back and allowed her robe to open. He tried to avert his eyes but it was the first time he had seen a woman's naked breasts or her forbidden triangle, and he could not. He was terrified, but he was also riveted. His affliction returned but he had no umbrella, only shame. Kathy said, "Nayif, we are two sides of the same coin. You want something from me, and I want something from you."

With some naïvete, but not very much, Nayif asked, "What is it that you want?"

"I will show you, Nayif. I will show you." She touched him in his affliction, and he tried to move away, but he couldn't. He couldn't. It was over in an instant, and he was mortified. Kathy looked at him with some amusement. This was better than she had imagined. "Are you a virgin?" she asked.

"Of course," Nayif replied, " I must wait for my wedding night to do such things."

"Nayif, if we are to do business together, we must be friends. Come with me." Nayif believed he was trapped. He needed Kathy to bring home the deal. For the King and for Allah, he would have to sacrifice himself.

Kathy was a masterful teacher. It was what she did best. At first, Nayif was a hesitant and self-conscious beginner, but soon he became a quick study, then an eager participant, and finally a ravenous animal. Nayif could not get enough of Kathy, and Kathy, worldly-wise as she was, could not get enough of Nayif. It was as if the years of deprivation stored up inside of him were just waiting to be unleashed in wild fury, and this innocent passion touched something deep inside of Kathy that she had not known for a very long time.

From Friday night until Monday morning, over and over again, each was consumed by the other. Nothing existed beyond their craving for fulfillment; nothing was more electrifying than the rapture of release, and nothing was more pleasurable than the tranquil intervals of half-sleep. Deep in his heart, Nayif knew that nothing would ever be the same, and for the moment, Kathy believed that she had regained her own soul.

Chapter 39

It was Friday afternoon and with everything under control for the weekend, Sally prepared to leave a little early. For the past month she had established this pattern, and with Feld's blessing, it seemed to be working out pretty well. She poked her head into his office, and said, "I'm taking off now, Feld. You know where to find me if you need me."

Feld replied, "Don't worry. Just get some rest. Our baby is getting bigger, and you need to take as much time off as you can. Sophie can do more, you know, and I can fill in." She had become a second daughter to him, and he got up from his desk, put his arm around her shoulder, and gave her a fatherly peck on the forehead.

When Sally left, he walked over to the window and waited. The valet parker usually brought the car to the front entrance, and he liked to watch until she was out of sight.

As Sally walked toward her car, three men in hooded windbreakers grabbed her, swept her into a white panel truck, held a chloroform-doused cloth over her nose and mouth until she passed out, and placed a blindfold on her eyes. They pulled away with their wheels screeching and turned left at the corner. Feld lost no time. In minutes, Griff, the local police, the Capitol police, and the FBI converged at the Washington Post.

The doorman and the valet parker described the vehicle. The panel truck was ditched in an alley less than three squares away where Sally had been transferred to a black limousine. Onlookers who sensed something wrong was happening had the good sense to check the license plate and report it. News bulletins were immediately posted on the Web and on TV.

On Saturday, Feld ran the story on the front page with a recent photo of Sally. On Sunday, even though the paper had been put to bed earlier, he held the presses and ran the story again. Griff was deluged with calls offering to help. Sally knew just about everybody in town, and it became obvious how well liked and respected she was. The big newspapers ran the story on their front-page, and multi-media photojournalists, cable networks, bloggers and other online Web specialists gave the story eyeballs. The rest of the print press and other online players also gave it everything they had.

When the all-points bulletin went out, Montgomery County Police Chief Duke Connelly remembered how nice Sally had been to him at the Ainsley place and thought he'd better keep an eye out just in case she landed in his jurisdiction. Black limos were pretty ordinary in his neck of the woods, and he had seen a few out on River Road this afternoon. He would follow up.

Sally was driven up River Road, two lanes past Fox Meadow to the destination. Accompanied by Madam X, she was carried up a narrow staircase to a small windowless room that was sparsely furnished with a large bed, a bedside table and a small chair. The blindfold was removed, and they laid her down on the bed.

Just to be sure Sally was okay, Madam decided to stay with her until she slept off the chloroform. She didn't like this job one bit. She didn't mind letting them bug her rooms and she liked precious diamonds, but she hadn't known the bugs might lead to murder. It was a good thing that she didn't know for sure. She and Ainsley had known each other for years, and they were fond of each other. In fact, in the early years, they were very fond of each other. They had assured her they would not hurt Sally. They just needed her for a while until the President released the Saudi Nighthawk sale and approved the Iranian economic package. Just a little blackmail is all it was. They held her illicit activities over her head, and she felt as much a victim as Sally. No, she didn't like this one bit!

Chapter 40

King Khalid tried to reach Prince Nayif on Friday, Saturday, Sunday, and Monday morning. He was livid.

Nayif picked up the newspapers that were strewn at his doorstep, glanced at the headlines and tried to dismiss the thought that somehow the Kingdom was involved. It wouldn't be the first time they had used a heavy hand when a light touch might have been more useful.

There were multiple messages waiting for him on his hard line. A weekend barrage of messages was highly unusual, especially since some were from the King and some from his father. He had ignored his cell until now, and there were multiple messages left for him there too.

He listened to the messages, which began in an urgent tone, escalated to an ominous tone, and ended with a direct threat to his very existence. He knew there was no way to escape his Uncle's ire. He had beheaded men for lesser sins. Maybe he could buy some time, but he figured he was a dead man. If he told the truth he was a dead man. If he concocted some story, it wouldn't hold up, and he was still a dead man. If he ran, they would find him. If he holed up, they would find him. Kathy had given him a key, and he figured his best shot was to hide out at her place. Maybe he could have a little more time with her before they caught up with him. It was worth a try.

Nayif threw some things into a duffle, grabbed the newspapers and hightailed it back to Kathy's. At Kathy's, he closed the mini-blinds, took a deep breath and sat down to read everything he could find on the Sally Burton story, and then turned on the computer to catch up on the latest. It had become an international story, and there was plenty to read and the more he read, the more he sweated. It was clear to him exactly who was playing this dangerous chess game. Only two crazed old men accustomed to wielding absolute power in a world that no longer needed anything they had to offer, would turn to such a hotheaded and foolish scheme. How was he going to survive this madness?

Both the King and the Iranian President were holding frequent full court press availabilities. Both offered effusive expressions of concern for the kidnapping of an influential American and in the same breath, they lamented that they had great compassion for this American woman in spite of America's poor treatment of them. His Royal Highness and President Faredi claimed they were praying to Allah to keep her safe. Then they would go on at great length about the double dealing on the economic package and the Nighthawk sale. They also made sure that rumors went out on You Tube that Sally had been kidnapped by the foreign agents of countries that had been double-crossed by the United States. Editorials were proliferating, pointing the finger at Saudi Arabia and Iran and no denials were made.

Nayif called Kathy on her private line, outlined the story and asked her to say nothing about his whereabouts. She told him to sit tight, and they would figure it out when she got home. Kathy quickly realized this was a very big deal. She took care of some pressing deadlines and headed home.

The kidnapping had horrified Kathy and after Nayif's call, she was downright scared. Until now she had spent a lot of energy avoiding personal entanglements. She had worked her butt off to get straight A's in college, and waited tables to pay her way. She managed to be second in the D.C. bar exam and her high rating landed her a top job on the Hill. She was not going to throw it all away on a whim.

Nayif was sitting on the edge of the sofa, anxiously waiting for Kathy. He got up quickly and rushed to embrace her but she stiffened and pushed him away. "Look, Nayif, we had a great weekend and I'll never forget it, but it's over. I'm not getting involved in this mess. You can hide out here for a day or two, but after that you've got to find someplace else to go. I don't have any room in my life for trouble, and sweetie, you are serious trouble. Who are these monsters? What the hell are they trying to accomplish? Somehow, Nayif, you have to let them know that it's a dead end street they are on. They have got to let Sally Burton go. She is a very big muck-a-muck and her kidnapping was a very big mistake. I can tell you this, Nayif, you had better warn them to keep her safe. They are in way over their heads. I may be crazy, but I won't turn you in yet. Two days, Nayif. That's all I can give you. After that, you're fair game."

Nayif's head was spinning. This was his only avenue of escape. He needed some sleep. Then he would decide where to go, but he thought he could never go home. Home meant the hellfire.

Chapter 41

Griff's phones at home and work and Feld's phones at the paper had been hooked up to police listening posts. A secure gathering spot had to be established but Sally's house was too small and too exposed to fit the bill. After lots of back and forth, the decision was made to set up at the Foster place on P Street. The location was easy to protect; there was plenty of space; Griff's parents were away at the mid-point of a 58-day South American cruise; and it was conveniently located for everybody.

Friday, Saturday, Sunday and Monday had passed with no contact from the kidnappers. It was hell for Griff. His old cravings were surging, the familiar watering of his mouth, the incessant thoughts of the taste, the persistent yearning for oblivion, but he grabbed his stalking tiger firmly by its tail. He locked the liquor cabinet, asked the head of the security detail to hold the key, and kept a Kool-aid drink in his hand. He needed to stay sober for Sally, for their unborn child and for Amos who had shown so much faith in him. He couldn't mess up now.

Raj and Jimmy Wu checked in and told Griff they were exploring their own contacts. Jimmy Wu said he had some ideas, and if they amounted to anything he'd be in touch. At the same time, unbeknownst to anyone but himself, Chief Connelly was investigating black limousines.

Madam was horrified by the non-stop press coverage. On all the cable networks, two phone numbers and a web site flashed constantly on the bottom of the screen. This was much more than she had bargained for. If anything went wrong, she could find herself in the hot seat and what for? She had cultivated influential friends, and in over twenty years of illicit activities, she had managed to stay out of trouble. This situation wasn't even any of her business. This high profile lady was very pregnant and Madam personally tried to make sure she was well fed and cared for, but Sally was listless, didn't talk much, ate very little, and slept or pretended to sleep much of the time.

Madam was becoming more agitated by the day. What if Sally went into labor? What if she needed special care even before then? This was insane. What were they thinking? What would become of her if she turned Sally in? She knew too much. She knew about the King's listening devices and cameras. She knew the faces of the King's men who collected the tapes and inserted new ones. She knew the face of the computer geek who managed the others. She knew Amir.

The investors, and she suspected they were merely mouthpieces for the King, insisted that Amir serve as her houseman and that the King's toadies be allowed to wire her rooms. Madam was well compensated, but she knew much more than she wanted to know. She would wait this out for now, but there was no way she would endanger Sally's life or let her lose this baby.

On Tuesday, Madam was sitting in Sally's room, just sitting there quietly, trying to get Sally to eat more of the lunch she had brought for her- a cream soup, a nice salad with grilled salmon and a glass of skim milk. Sally picked at it only because she knew she had to have some nourishment. The baby was so active, kicking, moving, and maybe turning; Madam could actually see the movement. She wanted to touch that baby, but she thought Sally must think of her as the enemy, and she didn't dare. She was staring at Sally's belly and Sally sensed Madam's curiosity. She said, "Would you like to feel the baby kicking?" She took Madam's hand and guided it onto a spot on her belly that was bulging. The baby moved and Madam was transfixed. This was the first time in her life she had felt such a thing. It warmed her hardened heart and it touched her mislaid soul.

Madam was born in Shanghai, a city of 12 million people that was almost bursting at the seams. In the midst of millions of refugees who had fled intolerable conditions in the countryside, Madam, then known as Zhang Li, was born on a sidewalk in the slums of the Putuo District. Her family was already eight in number, two parents, three grandparents, an aunt and uncle and their boy baby. They lived in two stacked 6x8 rooms, and there was no place to give birth in the confines of that tiny house. Most of the houses on the zigzag street looked like building blocks carelessly set by a small child, and Li was born under the eaves of one of them.

Li's own ramshackle house was located in a crooked passageway where no ray of sunshine ever found a path. There was no running water, no toilet, no indoor kitchen, no privacy and no hope. Between them, the women of the house owned one iron wok, one metal spatula and a one burner stove that they set on a pile of rubble for cooking. They tried to do their work without stepping in the sewage, which oozed like swollen rivers through the narrow alleys. At night, Li could hear the rats come in noisy armies to slurp the alleys clean. She didn't mind the sound for it meant that the next day she could find a clean place to squat.

To escape from her surroundings, Li went to school whenever she could. The slums in the next sector were being torn down but her school still stood amidst the wreckage. In school, Li learned some English and loved her English vocabulary book best of all.

In the winter of her 12th year, Li got sick with a bronchial cough, runny eyes and sharp pains in her ears. Her mother took her to see the doctor, who was not really a doctor, but a medicine man who made his money in the drug trade, but in penance and self-interest, he tried to do whatever he could for these impoverished people. He gave Li some cough syrup, eardrops, and aspirin for her fever and told her to return in one week.

The medicine man was quite taken by Li's loveliness. Her body was developing into a young woman's body with small pointy breasts, a tiny waist, and slim and shapely legs that gave rise to a suggestive sway in her walk. Her round face held wide set dark eyes, apple cheeks and soft well-shaped lips. The medicine man had an obligation to his trader to provide one girl a month in lieu of cash, and he thought Li was a perfect choice. He spoke to Li's mother of a better life for her daughter in America. He could arrange it. Li's parents could then have another child, perhaps a boy child who would take care of them in their old age.

Li put her few belongings into a homemade knapsack and with great anticipation for the good life she had seen on her walks into the fancy neighborhoods nearby, she walked away from the Putuo slum without a backward glance. The medicine man handed her off to his trader, and Li was escorted to New York on a cruise ship where her training began.

The New York Madam found her easy to handle, compliant, even appreciative. Li earned her trust and was permitted to do errands on her own. In this big city she could walk in the rain on sidewalks that glistened, buy whole melons, wear dresses that were made of single cloth, and never go hungry. She always returned to Madam because that was her home. There she could light up her room with the touch of a switch, take hot showers, use a flush, brush her teeth with a toothbrush and toothpaste, use her own haircomb, take English courses on her own computer and sleep in her own bed. Madam favored her with good customers, and she was happy to oblige them. She needed no encouragement, no drugs. To her, this was the good life.

When Li was 22, Madam died, everything changed, and she left for Washington to join some girls she knew who had already settled there. By now, she was highly regarded in the trade and earning big fees. She saved her money, bought a secluded house and soon she was managing other girls and making more money. Foreign investors came to her and put her in this mansion in Potomac where her elegant girls serviced the most influential men in the area. Each girl had a stylish suite of rooms, each girl dressed in designer fashions, each learned to be informed and interesting, and each spent hours, even days, entertaining their regular customers in this posh hideaway.

Now, tucked away in an attic room of this isolated place, Madam was led by Sally's hand to touch her swollen belly and to feel the innocent life growing inside her. She could feel a tiny baby, a little hand that seemed to reach out to her, and her heart grew soft. She felt a powerful emotion unknown to her until this moment.

She had come a very long way from the slums of Shanghai, and for somebody else's folly she could lose everything. No, she didn't like this one bit. Madam knew enough about American law to know she could be in deep trouble if her part in Sally's kidnapping ever surfaced. Crossing state lines was a big enough burden in her normal business. She had taken that gamble because the isolated and unlikely setting minimized the risk. But this, this was over the top.

Chapter 42

P Street was clogged with cars - local police cars, unmarked cars, a police van, private cars, black vans, and TV video trucks. Local residents were inconvenienced but most of them didn't complain. They understood the seriousness of the unfolding story. Some of them knew Griff from the time he was a little boy in knee-highs and his All Saints uniform, and they went to church to light a candle and pray for Sally's safe return. Some of them knew about his troubles and prayed he wouldn't fall off the wagon. Some were new in the neighborhood but their hearts went out to Griff, and to Sally whose fascinating columns they had followed for years.

Neighbors brought casseroles and cakes with notes attached offering help, prayers and suggestions, and handed them to the agents who were guarding the front gate. Griff read each one and wrote thank you notes to pass the time. He couldn't do anything more demanding than that.

Jimmy Wu checked in and said he was working on something that might just pan out, but he didn't have anything specific enough to pass on. With Griff's ok, Raj came by and sat by quietly in case Griff wanted to talk. Chief Duke Connelly spoke to the FBI to report that he was following up on some limousine leads in his neck of the woods, and he would stay in touch.

Celeste and Betsy called in often and spoke to the on-site lieutenant but didn't want to scare Griff with their near hysteria. These days, the two of them spent much of their time together trying to keep from going off the deep end, and Charles and Amos did their best to be supportive.

Feld kept a constant vigil at the office. If he forgot to check in with Sarah every few hours, she checked in with him. He made sure no edition went to press without a big story about Sally. He personally updated the Post's web pages and set up call-ins and emails for public response. Every day, there were hundreds of hits on sightings and suggestions. All of them were turned over to the FBI, and the promising ones were followed up.

Sally was not forgotten, not for an instant, and no people were more aware of this than Zhang Li and Nayif.

Chapter 43

With urgent business to discuss, His Royal Highness King Khalid anxiously awaited the imminent visit of Iranian President Farid Zahedi. Since he had bent his own rule and journeyed to Tehran for their first meeting, it was fitting that this time Farid was coming to him. He gave permission for Farid to arrive at the Royal Terminal of King Khalid Airport in Riyadh, where he was greeted by the Foreign Minister and accompanied to the Royal Palace.

The President was duly impressed as he walked through the vaulted entrance. The entrance walls were clad with large squares of highly polished Italian marble, illuminated with brilliant white sidelights. Glittering crystal chandeliers hung from the grand hall ceiling with their mirror images reflected on the dark marble floor. He was escorted into a lavish meeting room, more lavish than his own, and he was left there to wait for the King. A courtier brought in some refreshments on a solid gold tray bearing the emblem of the Royal Court. The President nibbled at them, but he was growing more agitated by the minute. How dare the King keep him waiting! Had he no respect for the President of a place much older and wiser than his own? Hadn't he treated the King with great respect when they met in Tehran?

The King entered; shooed away the Foreign Minister, and they were alone. Only the King and Farid remained. They kissed three times, once on each cheek and back again, and after the essential pleasantries, the King spoke excitedly, "My nephew, Prince Nayif, is nowhere to be found. No one else in Washington can do our business. Nayif knows the President. Nayif knows Foster. Nayif is necessary to our plan, and Nayif has disappeared. When I finish with this ingrate, he will be firewood for the hellfire! He will be sent to the lowest depths of the fire where there shall be no helper for him. I shall take the sword to this idiot. He shall suffer eternal damnation, but first, he must do our bidding. Your man, Mahmood, must locate him. He is a novice, but he can do this. They work closely together; he must have some idea of Nayif's whereabouts".

"Mahmood is a fast learner," replied Farid, "He can do more than you think. I will instruct him to find Nayif. The woman is heavy with child, and we must finish quickly."

The Foreign Minister made inquiry to Mahmood by text message. Finally, they were paying some attention to him. Mahmood did indeed have an idea of Nayif's whereabouts. He had been roaming the halls near Kathy Asher's office on the day Nayif was to meet with her. It was not coincidental. Nayif had informed Mahmood of this meeting, and Mahmood was curious. He hadn't wanted Nayif to go solo on this mission when they had agreed to partner, but he understood that Nayif thought he stood a better chance to uncover the holdup if he worked the Nighthawk issue one on one with Asher. Still, he did not trust Nayif. How could he? Prince Nayif was a Saudi.

"Enemies may be temporary," Mahmood said to himself, " but our differences are permanent. How dare the Un-Islamic Saudi Monarchy believe they are the keepers of the Holy Mosques of Mecca and Medina when they sacked our shrines in years past, and they cavort unashamedly with the Great Satan! Someday we shall destroy these inbred rulers of the Arabian Peninsula, and we shall lead them all. Then Iran shall be the center of an Islamic awakening that shall spread to every corner of the globe."

"It is true we also do business with the Great Satan, but we are simply twisting them in the wind while we bide our time. My country is a nuclear power now, and we shall strike when the iron is hot. When they let down their guard, we shall penetrate their shield, and in the first blow, we shall annihilate Israel and take back our Muslim land. Then we shall break America and overturn their heretic laws and sharia law shall become the law of their land. In our Revolution, we fought off the Great Satan of Western imperialism while the Saudis bedded them, and with the wisdom granted to us by Allah, blessed be He, we shed Western influence and shaped foreign policies of our own. We are an ancient Persian civilization, and the day comes soon when we shall take our rightful place as the true world leader. Inshallah."

"I work in America, and I work with Nayif because that is my job, but I do not have to like it." Mahmood's passionate soliloquy made his heart race and his brow sweat. He sat for a while to calm himself and then sent a text message of reply to the Foreign Minister.

Chapter 44

Chief Connelly checked out the van's D.C. license plate and it proved to be a long discarded one that led nowhere. A buddy of his at the D.C Police Department and he cooperatively checked the film of the traffic cameras that were scattered along the routes from the Washington Post on 15th Street into his jurisdiction, hoping for some clue on the limo. All but one checked out okay.

A camera on River Road picked up a blurred shot of a limo that showed the same two last numbers as the report provided by the bystanders. He ran a check of every limo owner in Montgomery County and came up dry. Each one had a legitimate license and could account for the whereabouts of the limo at the time of the kidnapping. All the limos were accounted for except for the limo with the blurred numbers. The film was sent to the FBI lab for further study.

Jimmy Wu was on the phone, the blogs and his computer non-stop. Something hung there in the back of his mind, but he couldn't bring it into focus, something linking a member of the Saudi Royal family to a local Chinese woman, something he had heard in passing. Where had he heard it, and what had he heard? He was hoping for some piece of information that would jar his memory.

The FBI was chasing down some leads, but they led up blind alleys and dead ends. Sally had disappeared into thin air.

Griff had his cravings, often felt frayed around the edges, wasn't getting much sleep, but considering the circumstances; he was hanging in there. The calming presence of his old friend Raj helped a lot and the constant concern of his neighbors and friends helped, too. Griff was grateful that a restless Feld kept the print press and the wireless communications going non-stop, and that his relentless leadership kept the story front page, top of the broadcast, and all over the Web. Sarah kept busy knitting baby sweaters and caps, baking for Griff and the agents and calling Feld whenever her emotions began to spin out of control. After Melanie, she and Feld wanted more children and never did anything to interfere with it happening, but it never did, and now she was personally and deeply attached to Sally and this new baby.

The Fosters heard the news on the TV in their posh suite on the Crystal Harmony and had the Captain arrange passage home for them out of their next stop in Santiago. They had grown quite fond of Sally and at the thought of being grandparents. They had waited a long time for this event, and they wanted to be there to support Griff. They had no doubt Sally would be found. They thought it was just a matter of money, and they wanted to be sure Griff had all he needed. They would see to it.

Amos Jackson was furious. Zahedi and Khalid kept up the drumbeat of their interest in the affair, and they were none too subtle. They were now claiming in the same voice that they had heard rumors of Sally's whereabouts. At each frequent press-availability, they mentioned the pending Nighthawk sale and the languishing economic package. The linkage was clear to Amos just as it was intended to be. Amos tried to reach Nayif to no avail. Where in the hell was he? He put some wheels in motion to locate him. He wanted to question Nayif before he made a diplomatic blunder that could have repercussions in the region. The last thing he wanted to do was undermine the progress of the past decade.

Much of the Middle East had changed. The more enlightened leaders of the region had succeeded in easing the pain of an impoverished people whose culture once had flourished and whose injured pride had driven them to rage and resentment. Many of these Gulf nations had modernized and were America's friends and trading partners, and Amos felt he had to protect these relationships with all the tact he could muster. The Saudi Royals and the Iranian Ayatollahs still espoused extremist beliefs, and the Iranian leaders continued to harbor visions of Persian Gulf supremacy and world domination. However, the Iranian people and their government were a world apart, and the Saudi people, discontented with their government's impending economic collapse, were moving away from puritanical and militant Sunni Wahhabism and beginning to look outward toward the developed world.

Iran's nuclear weapons still posed a clear and present danger to the region but with America's defensive missile shield in place and Iraq serving as a stable buffer, the Iranian government was effectively blocked from threatening their Gulf neighbors or extending their reach beyond the region. Amos couldn't afford to shake things up with mistaken accusations against the Saudis and the Iranians. If they weren't behind Sally's kidnapping, perhaps this was precisely what they wanted him to do. Even if this was crude mafioso-like blackmail to move the Nighthawk sale and the economic package, Amos had to be careful. But he had no intention of playing dead.

Mahmood responded to the Saudi Foreign Minister's inquiry and reported on Prince Nayif's movements on the day he had followed him. He had been incensed by Nayif's un-Islamic behavior and Mahmood's observations were laced with more than a tinge of ill feeling. His Persian Shia sensibilities told him he could not expect more of an Arab, especially a blasphemous Sunni. He gave an account of Nayif's time with Kathy Asher in the coffee shop, of his walk to her house and of the vigil Mahmood kept there until he gave up waiting for Nayif to reappear. The trail ended at about midnight when Mahmood left the scene and drove home. Kathy's address was included in his message to the Minister.

Chapter 45

Madam was frenzied. There were bills to pay and her girls hadn't worked for a week. Sally was becoming more and more lethargic. There had been no contact from the elusive kidnappers, and she had no specific knowledge of who they were. All of the arrangements had been made through Amir and her frequent questions extracted only shrugs. She had Sabir's wireless number but he had been very clear that she was to call him only in a dire emergency. Well, what was this? Sally was not getting less pregnant! The media were not getting less out front. The police agencies were not slowing their investigation. In fact, the longer this went on, the more the public was getting involved. New call-in numbers were posted. New search groups were being formed, and more college and high school groups were fanning out in spider web formation beginning at the place where Sally was thrown into the limo into all of the District, Maryland, and Virginia. Madam was left with no choice but to take the bull by the horns. But how! She couldn't speak inside without being picked up by a bug. She couldn't leave the house without giving Amir a good excuse. How?

As for Sally, the stress was becoming unendurable. In the beginning, she tried to keep her thoughts positive by focusing on the baby and keeping her head busy. She thought up stories and tried to memorize them. She thought up a story about making bad choices because the main character wasn't mature enough to make good ones, about looking back with clearer eyes and finding that even in the worst of times, there were good times. She tried to think up a feature story about the kidnapping, but she couldn't find a handle for it. It just didn't make sense.

Creating these stories in Sally's head kept her from going crazy and so did the little kindnesses that Li bestowed upon her. Li tried to please her with food she liked, with walks up and down the short hallway, with an exercise routine, with pleasant conversation and with genuine interest and concern for the baby. After a few days everything began to look upside-down. Sally had begun to feel that Li was her friend and protector. When she got back to the paper maybe she would initiate a series on brainwashing.

Li was spending more time with Sally, revealing parts of her childhood, not all of it, but enough so that Sally's silent stories began to include stories about Li. Sally confessed her fear to Li of going into labor in this isolated room and suddenly the floodgates opened and she burst into tears. Li took her into her arms and held her until the tears stopped, but Sally needed something more. A quiet voice inside told her to turn to God for help, but how could she pray if she had no words?

During her small town Iowa childhood she had obediently gone to the Methodist church every Sunday with her mother, Melba, a pretty woman who waitressed long hours, never laughed, never wore even a hint of makeup and always dressed in drab colors. At least, that was the way Sally remembered it.

When Sally was eight years old her mother told her that her good-looking, hardworking and usually silent father had gone on a fishing trip with his buddies. As far as Sally knew, Melba never saw or heard from him again. When Sally realized he was probably gone for good, she sobbed into her pillow every night for months, certain that she had done something terrible to make him leave.

A talented writer and an award-winning editor of her high school paper, Sally left home on a full scholarship to Columbia and never returned to her hometown or to her church. She sent a greeting card and phoned her mother twice a year, on her mother's birthday and on Mother's Day, and Melba sent Sally a birthday card and a Christmas card. She tried hard to bring Melba's face into focus, but she couldn't.

Sally was losing control but for the baby's sake she knew she had to regain it. All that mattered now was this baby. She had to find a way to hang on to something bigger than herself, bigger than this room, bigger than her fear, something to protect her sanity, something to safeguard this precious life growing inside her. She tried to remember a Sunday school psalm that helped her through her childhood troubles and some of the words rushed into her mind, "Merciful God, we cry out to you in our trouble and we pray that you lead us out of our trouble; and Almighty God heard their plea and brought them out of their trouble and brought them out of their distress. He stilled the storms to a whisper and He hushed the waves of the sea." The words quieted her tremors and in the stillness she remembered the song her Sunday school class sang every year at the school pageant, trying their best to do in unison the endearing little motions they had rehearsed all year. Recalling the song and the sweet young girls and boys who sang it, brought comfort to Sally's anxious heart:

The light of God surrounds me,
The love of God enfolds me,
The power of God protects me,
The presence of God watches over me,
And wherever I am, God is.

Soon she found her own words and Sally began a personal conversation with God that would continue for a lifetime. Sitting in that lonely bed in that little room without windows, she prayed for a long time until a white light entered her space and she felt encircled by it. Embraced by the warmth of the light, Sally surrendered her future to the outstretched arms of fate.

Li witnessed Sally's passage from anguish to serenity, and she was deeply moved by it. She didn't know what to call it, but she was sure it was something holy. Somehow, Li was going to free her. No matter what harm it would bring to her, she was not going to continue this madness. She was not going to be a partner in something that put her in league with Mara, the Buddhist devil. She was going to be careful, but she was going to take a chance and call Sabir.

Chapter 46

Nayif had nowhere to turn. He knew he was trapped. On day two, Kathy told him in no uncertain terms that his time was up. He had to leave. He kept the TV and talk-radio on and constantly scanned the blogosphere. The coverage of Sally's kidnapping was relentless, and it was clear to him and to everybody else that there was a strong link to the Saudis and the Iranians. Their leaders were behaving like madmen, like children having temper tantrums, and he would surely be their scapegoat. Even his father could not save him from the King's rage nor could he shield him from his legendary sword. His only shot was to turn himself in and ask for political asylum.

Kathy got through to Griff, whom she knew and had done business with over the years. Under cover of darkness, Griff, two FBI agents and a CIA operative came and spirited Nayif away just ahead of the Saudi Foreign Minister and his entourage's arrival on Kathy's doorstep. The agents, who were adamant that Kathy needed some protection until they could scope things out, took her with them.

The Foreign Minister and his aides had arrived only minutes too late. In panic, they rang the doorbell over and over again. With no information for his King, the Minister knew he was in serious trouble. He returned to the Embassy, kneeled on his prayer rug and begged the Prophets for Intercession. He had a good life here on Earth, and if he died with dishonor he would surely burn in the hellfire.

The agents decided that the Foster house in Georgetown was as good a spot as any to use as Headquarters Central for Nayif's holding place. They had set up their paraphernalia there, and the house was large enough to isolate him for interrogation. They set up an interrogation room on the third floor, which went smoothly because Nayif willingly, even eagerly gave up whatever information he had.

Agents searched Nayif's apartment and Kathy's place, and they brought a cardboard box of papers they had gathered and went through them with Nayif piece by piece. They checked his cell records and tracked the King and Sabir's rash of calls to him. The calls indicated panic and the timing coincided with Sally's kidnapping.

They guided Nayif back to his activities of the past year, to his lobbying, to his visits back home, to his relationships with Mahmood, with Kathy, with his father, with the King. He didn't mention his errand to deliver a gift to the Asian lady because it simply hadn't occurred to him that it was of any importance. It was just an errand.

A scrap of paper with a phone number and directions scribbled on it was extracted from the box – River Road, two lanes past Fox Meadow, left to the end of the lane to a big white house. Nayif explained the errand the King had assigned to him, including the fact that his father had provided the directions. He described his visit and the strangeness of the house. The agents knew that this warranted immediate follow up and with Nayif in tow, they went downstairs to report the lead. After a quick conference, the charge agent called Chief Connolly, alerted him to the situation, and arranged to converge at a shopping center on River Road. In the meantime, the Chief blocked the intersection of the lane and River Road and the FBI sent a helicopter to overfly the house and keep an eye on it. As a precaution, an ambulance was called and told to pull into the lane and wait. Griff, Nayif, four FBI agents and two CIA agents left in two unmarked cars with silent red light flashers affixed to the car roofs. They met up with Connelly who had four police cars plus a Chief's car lined up and waiting.

In the meantime, Li told Amir she was getting claustrophobia staying in that small room with Sally, that she was feeling nauseous and needed to get some fresh air. She assured him that Sally was napping and that she had locked the door to Sally's room. She just needed to take a walk for five or ten minutes to fill her lungs. She wouldn't leave the grounds.

Once outside, she found a spot under the eaves where she could not be seen from the house. She called Sabir who warned her that she could be in grave danger. Sabir knew that Amir was the King's man and that the King might have concocted this crazy scheme, but he assured Li that he had no part of it.

"I am relieved that Sally is safe, but I fear for her, and for you and Nayif. My brother has gone mad. He has held unchecked power for too many years and now that he is losing it, he is also losing his mind. Zahedi isn't helping the situation because he is in a panic too."

King Khalid had known all along of Sabir's strong ties to Li. In fact, he had made use of them from time to time. Sabir explained to Li that he had tried to fly out of his retreat in the Allawz Mountains, but the King's Guards stopped him and were keeping him prisoner in his own chalet.

"I suppose the King," Sabir said, "wants to hold all the aces until he wins this crazy hand he's playing."

His voice tremulous with anger, Sabir said, "Li, you must get help at once. Sally must be freed. Whatever the consequences, we will face them together."

With trembling fingers, Li dialed the emergency police number, told them where to find Sally and rushed back inside. The call was immediately forwarded to the Chief.

Jimmy Wu called in and was told by an agent that Griff had left the house. Jimmy said he was getting warm. Some leads were pointing to a connection between a Chinese woman and the Saudi Crown Prince, but he hadn't been able to identify the woman yet. He was working the phones.

When Li returned to the house, Amir was gone. She wondered what had tipped him off to leave, but she was glad that he had fled. One less problem to deal with! Sally and Li sat together quietly. Li felt a great sense of relief, and she wanted to share the news of what she had done, but she didn't want to excite Sally. She wasn't sure the excitement would be good for the baby. For now, she would simply sit with her and hold her hand.

It was dusk. The sun dropped swiftly behind the tree line and the pearl tinted moon came into view against the cloudless sky. Around the bend of the lane, the big house emerged in silhouette against the darkening horizon. More police vehicles sped up River Road, and Nayif assured the Chief that they had the right intersection. The cars joined the ambulance and formed a caravan. All the vehicles silenced their sirens and drove slowly up the narrow lane to the house. The helicopter pilot reported that there were lights in some of the windows of the house but no visible movement.

Li heard rustling sounds move across the rutted pebble drive and thought it would be safer for her and for Sally if she let the police know it was okay to enter. She told Sally she would return in a moment and went into the hall to contact them. Her message was relayed immediately to the Chief. He called Li and asked to speak to Sally. Li returned to the room and with tears in her eyes and a catch in her throat, she explained to Sally all that was happening. The Chief alerted Griff who emerged from the second car and rushed to the entrance. Li asked him if it would be safe for her to open the door. With his assurances, Li opened the front door. There were bright klieg lights and men all over the place, some with guns drawn, some with rifles. Li was shackled, and led them to Sally who was struggling on wobbly knees to make her way down the staircase.

Griff dashed up the stairs and swept Sally into his arms. He would never let her go. Never. The paramedics were right behind him. They made a basket of their arms and carried Sally to the foyer, insisting that she get on the stretcher for the ride to the hospital. Sally resisted but Griff assured her he wouldn't leave her side. She just needed to be checked out. As she was being wheeled out on the gurney, she asked the Chief to treat Li gently, that she was as much a victim as Sally, and she would not press charges. In fact, if there were a trial, she would testify for her.

"Small world, Chief. You and I seem to get together only when there is a crisis. How about we change that?"

The Chief's chest swelled and a broad smile spread across his weathered face, so wide that you could see black holes where his molars should have been. He patted Sally on the shoulder and said he was honored to serve her. The quaver in his voice and the hint of a tear in his eye told Sally that he really meant it. As far as the Chief was concerned, she was one of the "good people." She treated him as an equal and made him feel important. That meant a lot to him.

Amos arranged for Sally to be taken to the Presidential suite at the hospital, for her safety as well as for her comfort. Sally gave her gatekeeper, a beefy head nurse who looked like a defensive tackle and barked like a quarterback, a list of permitted visitors, mainly a circle of friends who had become her newfound family — Arthur and Pamela Foster, Celeste and Charles, Sarah and Feld, Amos and Betsy, Sophie, Raj Singh. They coordinated their visits with Griff so they wouldn't tire Sally. One by one, they came by with a Laurelwood bouquet of flowers, Sally's favorite Watergate Bakery's chocolate dipped strawberries, petit fours compliments of the senior White House baker, a scrapbook of Washington Post stories on the kidnapping in a big box that included a small box of apple strudel, and a few assorted and sundry baby things.

The strain of the past week left Sally feeling shaky, tiring easily, and after visitors left she slept like a baby. Griff sat at her bedside, holding tight to her hand, staring endlessly at her face and her growing belly, saying unfamiliar prayers of thanks to God for bringing her safely back to him. The prayers were awkward for him because he didn't know what he really believed, but he figured the prayers couldn't hurt and just in case there was an Almighty power helping Sally through this ordeal, he owed Him some gratitude.

Sally awakened from one of her naps in a foggy state and felt the comfort of Griff's hand in hers. With his other hand he reached into his pocket, retrieved a tiny steel grey box, and wordlessly handed to her. She looked up at him quizzically and opened the box. There was a smaller box inside, a black velvet box with a hinged lid. Griff grinned like a Cheshire cat as she gingerly opened the lid. Sitting there in the center of the small box was an exquisite oval sapphire stone surrounded by emerald cut tapered diamonds. It was the most beautiful ring Sally had ever seen. She raised an eyebrow, and in that flirtatious way that made Griff melt, she asked, "What did I do to deserve this?"

"Everything." Griff struggled to choke down the tears that threatened to flow and when he regained control his eyes met Sally's and his voice rose barely above a whisper. "You are everything to me, Sally. Before you, I had an empty place I couldn't fill and now you fill it. I love you, Sally, and I want to marry you and spend the rest of my life making you happy. I promise I'll never hold you too close and suffocate you. I'll give you space to grow, to be you own person. I'll never give you misery. I'm scared to death you won't trust love again. That's why I haven't asked sooner. I've just been too scared."

"Griff, I was trying to get up enough nerve to ask you. I love you, Griff. It's different this time. I know that. We're like two pieces of a puzzle. Apart we're just Rorschach inkblots. Together we make sense. Let's do it soon, before the baby comes. That will make Betsy and Celeste very happy. They've been driving me crazy."

Relief flooded his being and Griff laughed heartily. "On more than one occasion, my boss, the President of these United States, the most powerful man in the world, has sheepishly asked me if we were planning to set the date. I guess Betsy has been driving him crazy, too. By the way, he claims she wants us to marry in the White House. How does that strike you?"

"Celeste wants us to marry at Laurelwood. We might have to toss a coin."

"You girls are more than a guy can handle. I've been in agony, and you've been planning a wedding all along."

"Don't feel left out, Griff. We were going to invite you. Griff and Sally Foster. Sounds right, doesn't it?"

Chapter 47

The day after Sally's rescue, The Washington Post's front-page headline read:

BURTON IS BACK

Alleged Kidnapper Arrested and Claims Innocence

Maury Feld, with contributions from his top crime and political reporters, came into the bullpen, sat at a reporter's desk and personally wrote the four-column article. This time Feld wanted to feel the power and the pleasure of words with the naked flesh of his fingertips. It was his way of making Sally's return to the bosom of her family and friends feel real. The article began:

"Montgomery County Police Chief Duke Connolly announced the arrest of Zhang Li, a Chinese national and an alleged suspect in the abduction and captivity of Sally Burton, managing editor of the Washington Post. A material witness to the crime, Prince Nayif, son of Saudi Crown Prince Sabir turned himself in to Federal officials and is seeking political asylum. Although Prince Nayif is in no way implicated in the kidnapping, which began with three thugs who continue to be hunted, he was instrumental in leading officials to the scene of Burton's confinement.

A Saudi national whose name is known only as Amir, fled the crime scene and a manhunt for him is underway. A black Cadillac limousine, Maryland license AJ 1922 and a white panel truck are also being sought in connection with the kidnapping.

Last year, Saudi and Iranian nationals on tours of duty to their respective embassies, joined with homegrown American traitors in a thwarted espionage attempt to disrupt the nation's energy supply. It was purported by law enforcement agencies that U.S. Senator Winston Ainsley's assassination is connected to his heroic efforts to expose the attempt, and although his assailant died at the scene, it is believed that the crime has never been completely solved. Allegedly, strong suspicion is emerging that the Saudis and the Iranians were involved in Burton's kidnapping as well."

Feld went on to describe Sally's rescue, the place where she had been held, the known circumstances of her captivity and an update of her medical condition. He went into Sally's professional background, the Pulitzer Prize she had earned, and extolled her virtues with respect and affection.

The reporters who thought they knew Feld remarked with amazement that his veins obviously held more than ice water. Although Sarah, Melanie, Sally and his close friends already knew this, even Sarah was surprised when he broke down and cried like a baby. He was undone by the stress of the past week, his worry about Sally and the baby and his tireless efforts to keep Sally's kidnapping front and center.

Sarah, who had suffered deeply at the thought of losing Sally and the baby, quickly surrendered to her naturally less restrained emotions and joined him. They sat together on the sofa sobbing like the world had come to an end and then laughing because it hadn't.

Chapter 48

Upon learning from his agents of Heir Apparent Sabir's cell communication with Li, King Khalid ordered his arrest. He sent a contingent of his Royal Guards to Sabir's mountain lodge to take him into custody and bring him to the Palace in Riyadh. The word quickly spread through the vast network of 7,000 cousins, all of whom were descended from 18th century Muhammad ibn Saud. It was through the marriage of ibn Saud's son in 1744 to the daughter of Muhammad Abn al Wahhab that the more rigid and less tolerant practice of Islam known as Wahhabism was born. King Khalid was a strict follower of Wahhabism. Crown Prince Sabir was most definitely not. The cousins were divided in their beliefs and their loyalties, but they kept their counsel for now to see which way the wind would blow.

With the demand for oil disappearing and the Nighthawk sale buried, the years of the silent compact of Saudi oil for American guns and military equipment had come to a close. During the time of $200 and more a barrel, Khalid's more progressive predecessor had recognized the need to diversify the Kingdom's economy. He began to build modern cities and a metropolis on the Red Sea with factories, housing, resorts, commercial towers soaring to heights unsurpassed in the Persian Gulf, and a seaport to dwarf the seaport in Jeddah.

The market for Persian Gulf oil collapsed and the wind-blown desert sands covered construction sites like an undulating blanket of dust. With money and friends now in short supply, the rift between the monarchy and the people was widening by the day, with even the Royals increasingly divided. King Khalid and his followers were desperately trying to hold onto the levers of power while Sabir and many of his ruling class cousins were pulling further and further away.

Since the wealth of the Kingdom was an exclusively owned family asset, Sabir, like many of the Saud clan, was a very rich man. This largess had been distributed to him through direct allotments of crude oil to sell on the open market, huge land allocations and outright cash handouts. A born politician with good instincts and a generous disposition, Sabir built a mini kingdom of his own by widely sharing his fortune with lesser royals and commoners.

As a child Sabir was nurtured by British and Irish nannies. Over the years, they secretly regaled him and amused themselves with romanticized tales of fun and frolic. Their stories had him carousing with Parisian dancers in Montmartre, kicking up his heels with prima ballerinas in New York, waltzing with regal princesses in ballrooms in Vienna, and drinking beer with bar girls in Belgium. Sabir, in contrast to most of his huge family, had developed a thirst for Western ways before he ever stepped foot outside the confines of his own country.

During his college days at Brown University, the favored University of the higher echelon of the Saud Royal family, Sabir, an engaging fellow who spoke English with the charming linguistic inflections of his nannies, easily made friends. An articulate and very handsome fellow, a skillful lacrosse player, a champion rower and a big spender, he was one of the most popular men on campus.

Now, he would turn for help to two of his close college friends who lived in nearby Israel. With the aid of a network of loyalists at home and his friends in Israel, Sabir planned his escape from the clutches of his older brother. When the moon was only a thin sliver, Sabir's well-armed militia overtook the King's crack gang of Royal Guard warriors and spirited Sabir away to a neighboring field where a small private plane was waiting.

The plane carried Sabir from this field in the Allawz Mountains of Tabuk across Jordanian air space into a private airstrip in Israel. Upon his arrival, his friends met him — Gideon Alon, a Captain in the Shin Bet, and retired General Joshua Peretz, now a member of the Knesset. They came in a military vehicle accompanied by armed and ruddy looking Israeli soldiers who took off with steady speed towards a remote kibbutz in the Negev desert. It was the place where they would hide Sabir while they planned their next move. The sights Sabir saw in the Negev that day would have lasting impact on the lives of his own people.

Traveling the desert highway, Sabir saw ruins of ancient sites, busy outdoor-cafes in quaint towns and villages with chatty young people holding hands and sipping drinks, and occasional groups of artists busy painting desert sunsets and Jerusalem skylines. But most amazing to him, he saw endless fields of crops being watered by continuous rows of sprinklers, thousands of acres of greenhouses, clusters of date palms lining the roadways, colorful fruit and vegetable stands manned by people of all ages hawking their wares, and caravans of food trucks speeding toward their destination. How could this be?

If the Israelis could raise crops in this desert, why couldn't his people raise crops in theirs? Once they had made a half-hearted attempt to raise desert wheat, but the desert cannot be conquered with half-heartedness and the attempt had failed. Here in the Negev, more than eighty years had passed since rugged pioneers and shell-shocked survivors of the holocaust blended their sweat to turn this desert into an agricultural marvel. Here, out of the ashes of Auschwitz emerged technology giants and eager workers undaunted by hard labor, workers dedicated to defying senseless death by planting seeds of life.

In his kibbutz hideaway, Sabir's friends excitedly explained Israel's water carrier system, a network of underground pipelines, open canals, reservoirs and tunnels that brought water from the Sea of Galilee to the coastal region and then pumped it into the Negev. They also explained their advanced methods for purifying wastewater and for harvesting brackish desert water, and their groundbreaking ways of converting water from the seas into drinking water, even water from the very same Red Sea that lapped wave-by-wave onto the shores of Sabir's own land. Although the Saudis were not strangers to converting seawater into drinking water, perhaps a gift of these new conversion techniques and engineering designs for crop watering could be a steppingstone to friendship.

In words laced with passion, Alon and Joshua explained to Sabir that the Negev, an ancient desert wasteland once bereft of people, had become a fertile place alive with people, because big dreams and ingenuity and need had come together to make it so. "Here," Joshua said, "in the middle of the desert, blooming orchards and thriving nurseries sit alongside breeding lakes of giant sea bass and talapia, to mark the existence of a Jewish people once condemned to extinction. It is here, in this land of our ancestors, that we proclaim our survival." Now Sabir realized that he must find a way to instill this passion in Nayif, a way to give him the tools that would set him apart from all of the other pretenders and make him worthy of the throne. Perhaps advanced water technology would give Nayif something better than Nighthawks and more precious than oil to offer the Kingdom. If Nayif could bring fresh water to a parched desert and make it bloom, if he could breathe new life into a struggling economy, he would prove his value. It would take money and know-how and now Sabir knew where to find the know-how, and he had ideas about the money.

The Western educated Sabir also hoped that if Nayif worked with the Israelis in common cause, he could help mend the old tear that had split the Jews and the Muslims apart. The Jews were the source of the root and the Muslims were of the same root. In many places and for countless years, they had lived together in harmony and they could again. Sabir had a different life in mind for himself, but Nayif was young and smart and at the dawn of his. Making the Saudi desert bloom would give him a purpose greater than himself. It would help him leave a footprint in the same desert sands that were meant to be the place of his dwelling. Nayif and Aiaisha had a future, a future that did not include him. Sabir was content to know this is how it should be. He would find Nayif and then he would get Li out of the mess the frantic King and his equally frantic Iranian cohorts, had gotten her into.

During Sabir's four years as cultural attaché to his Embassy in Washington, Li was his tutor in the grown-up ways of love and friendship. She opened his eyes to places of the heart he had never known before. He owed her his awakening, and he would leave no stone unturned to free her. He understood deep in his gut that Li could never survive a prison akin to the prison of her childhood; that her very existence hinged on breathing fresh air. He had begun to realize that his did, too. He had grown apart from the insular lives of his three wives. They were content to remain in their respective palaces, to spend afternoons in the courtyard with their servants, to wear their abayas when they ventured outside with an escort, to still ask for written permission to see a doctor, to be owned lock, stock and barrel by the males in their lives. He had tried to give them freedom of movement. Since new laws had granted them the right to drive he had encouraged them to learn, but they were "old school" and they chose to keep the old ways. He would divorce them to free them, but he would see to it that they were well kept in the lives they had chosen. He had another path to walk.

Chapter 49

Griff brought Sally home to his parents place in Georgetown where she would be well protected by FBI agents until they were satisfied that she was out of danger. They had leads on the thugs who grabbed her and on the white panel truck they used for the job. The thugs bragged to drinking buddies in a bar about the ease with which they had earned $300 for a quick three-block ride to meet up with a limo. The bartender called in this tip anonymously in the first days of Sally's disappearance, suggesting these thugs were junkies looking for a fix. In the bar they had met up with a known dealer and according to the tipster, they left to do their deal outside. The agents were systematically checking out bars and white panel trucks. There were no leads on Amir who had vanished without a trace.

The Fosters spruced up a third floor guest suite for Sally and Griff, which Sally reached in the quaint two-person lift, housed behind the main stairs. For Sally's comfort the Fosters made the thoughtful gesture of placing an antique ice cream parlor chair in the corner of the lift. Sometimes the lift puffed and sputtered, and they explained that it would be safer for her and for the baby if she were sitting. They tried to give Sally and Griff privacy, but they couldn't resist a bit of hovering.

Then of course there was the matter of the wedding. The "girls" – Celeste, Betsy, with Pamela Foster and Sarah Feld now increasing their number, met endlessly on every detail imaginable and some unimaginable, to plan a "small" ceremony and just a "tad larger" reception. Sally was outnumbered, and at first she just surrendered. They were having such fun she didn't want to interfere.

Sarah, who was naturally shy, emerged from reticence on the topic of food, especially pastries; Celeste was the indisputable expert on flowers;

Betsy took on the role of invitations and logistics. Pamela lined up the family's Episcopal priest and brought in her Georgetown couturier to design and make Sally's dress. It was only when they conferred with her over the guest lists that Sally put her foot down.

"One hundred for the ceremony is not a small number. Thirty-five and no more! Not even the White House beagle! A "tad larger" for the reception is not 150. A "tad larger" is 75 tops. Same rule applies for the beagle! I have to admit though you are an impressive team of wedding planners, a little overwhelming for a small town girl from Iowa, but I'll handle it if you stick to the numbers."

The "girls" threw up their hands, shook their heads, and continued with their conspiratorial tea party. Sally smiled, satisfied that she had made her point. She headed for the lift with a high wave of her arms and went upstairs to take a nap.

Another day or so of this lazy life, and she was going back to work. She was beginning to long for the pursuit of the big "get," the adrenalin rush that comes with chasing deadlines, the cacophony of newsroom sounds, the collegial interplay with her reporters and even the absurdity of Feld's food deliveries. Safe on the outside or not, she was going to take her life back.

Chapter 50

The Mossad put out feelers on Zhang Li and Nayif's status and location. Their CIA compatriots wanted to know why in the world they were interested, but over the years they had learned to work in tandem and trust each other. They asked out of casual curiosity, not to blow them off.

As a member of Shin Bet, Captain Gideon Alon was assigned to domestic intelligence gathering, but Israel's continuing need for security for its people depended on linkages with the Mossad in Tel Aviv, whose foreign intelligence gathering capabilties were legendary.

Mossad's logo, "Everything Is Possible" said it all. With their army of cross-border agents and their well-documented ties to the CIA, NSA, the Pentagon, U.S. Homeland Security, and the Joint Counter Terrorism Office, it was child's play to find Nayif and pinpoint Li's position in the judicial system's pipeline. After they worked these priorities, Sabir wanted them to find the loose end that was the mysterious Amir.

Within an hour of the inquiry, Nayif's whereabouts and Li's situation were revealed in detail. Nayif was being held in protective custody at the Foster place until they could figure out what the heck to do with him. There was justifiable concern for Nayif's safety, and there was clatter that he might be moved to a hideaway sometimes used for U.S. government officials. Captain Alon arranged an important phone call and Sabir spoke at length to Nayif and to the other key players who could affect Nayif's travel to the Holy Land.

The Immigration and Customs Enforcement Agency (ICE) were holding Li in detention on charges that she had overstayed her legal status and a deportation hearing was pending. That was all the authorities had because Sally claimed that Li was being held against her will and refused to press charges, there were no witnesses to Li's long-standing misdeeds, the laptop was gone, and there was a curious but complete absence of records of any kind. Thus far, Li had managed to escape any criminal charges beyond the immigration issue, and Captain Alon used a light hand and a good contact to make sure it stayed that way.

Where Nayif was concerned, Sabir knew he had to get things right with his brother so that Nayif could return home. But first Nayif needed some time to gain the expertise and the connections that would give him the bargaining chips he needed to become a valuable asset to the Kingdom. Sabir was aware that Griff held the purse strings that could underwrite the water project, but he did not yet know that Nayif had established a strong friendship with Griff during his time at the Foster place.

Sabir also knew he needed to find a place in this world for Li, a place out of harms way where he could care for her as she had once cared for him. Deep inside he had always felt this pull, this feeling that their destiny was intertwined, that their relationship did not exist only in a fleeting moment in time, that her arms were not just a safe place where he could practice the Western ways that were a comfortable fit to his nature. He never felt this more than when they were apart, never more than the times when he tried to live an Islamic life with his three wives and the many children that he hardly knew. Nayif was his first child and the only one with whom he had established a lasting bond. After Nayif, there was Li, and he was ever after torn between two worlds, yet feeling he belonged to neither. Now he had to make peace with his foolish older brother, and see to it that Nayif became the new Crown Prince.

Chapter 51

Griff and Sally were betrothed in a wedding ceremony that took place in the informal atmosphere of the Solarium. Her flowing dove grey silk chiffon dress with silver satin edging was draped in layers that artfully concealed her growing belly. She held a wedding bouquet, painstakingly hand-tied by Celeste with French braided white ribbon intertwined with the white Singapore orchids that were grown by Charles in his beloved orchid greenhouse. The orchids were set off by deep plum and lavender angel face, meticulously selected by Celeste from her blooming gardens.

Sally was a veritable vision of loveliness, a living Renoir painting, and Griff's heart skipped a beat when he first saw her all put together. Just as Sally had insisted, there were only 35 guests for the ceremony. The Foster's Priest from the Georgetown Parish of St. John's Episcopal Church performed the ceremony in an abbreviated version leaving space for Sally and Griff to recite their more personal vows.

Looking into Sally's eyes, which held the hint of a tear, Griff took her trembling hand, and said, "Sally, for too long my wounded heart was closed to love. Then you walked right into my heart and you healed it. You renewed my life, and now my life belongs to you. You gave me your love and in return I give you all that I am or ever will be, and all that I have or ever will have. On this day, I make a solemn vow to respect you and to honor you, to love you truly and unsparingly, in good times and in bad times, in joy as well as in sorrow. You are my beloved, Sally, now and forever."

"Griff, wherever the wind blows, I will be there for you. I will love you until the trumpets call us home. Both of us have wandered through thickets and both of us have been bloodied by angry thorns. Yet we survived our trials because we were destined to be together. Together, Griff, we will build a dwelling strong enough to withstand winter storms and spacious enough to hold a busy life. It will be a place where we can grow as individuals, yet treasure our togetherness, a place where matters of the heart come before everything else. You are my beloved, Griff, now and forever."

With his eyes glistening, the Priest completed the marriage vows, and Sally and Griff, now husband and wife, knelt before him to receive his blessing.

Chapter 52

The reception for 75 guests was held in the Blue Room. The elegant wedding cake, which Sally courteously but firmly suggested be reduced from an extravagant 9 layers to a less extravagant 5 layers, sat in the center of the oval room on a round marble table under the Blue Room's renowned French cut-crystal and mahogany chandelier. The buffet tables were skirted in pale blue satin and held an elaborate display of fruits and cheeses, an array of wonderful cold finger foods and a seemingly endless line of silver chafing dishes attended by white-coated waiters but the dessert table was the standout. It displayed an array of the White House pastry chef's fancy signature pastries juxtaposed against Sarah's delicious miniature apple strudels, thumbprint butter cookies, and melt-in-your-mouth powdered sugar nut balls. Sarah stationed herself near the pastries so she could overhear the comments. Melanie, somewhat awed by the occasion, never left her mother's side.

With the enthusiasm that was natural for her, Betsy worked the room like the perfect hostess. For now, this was her White House, and what could be better than having such a happy occasion in it. She had grown to love Sally as the sister she had never had and felt particularly protective towards her since she was carrying the communal baby. Amos watched her and there was a tug in his heart because he was attuned to her thinking and he knew how much she had wanted a baby of her own. He hoped this shared baby would help to fill the emptiness.

Celeste and Charles roamed the room together, never more than inches apart. They seem to take nourishment from one another, occasionally putting a fingertip on a cheek, a hand at an elbow, brushing a stray hair from a brow, obviously smitten, obviously happy.

The Fosters were in their element. The White House was a venue they were comfortable in and most of the guests had been guests at one time or another at their own soirees. They floated from one to the other, skillfully engaging in the small talk that was "de rigueur" at standup receptions. They were so relieved that Griff and Sally had tied the knot before the baby came, and they were ecstatically happy that they were finally going to have a grandchild. They had worried about Griff but Sally seemed so right for him, they felt they could relax now. He was in good hands.

Feld was a contented man. Although his position in the Washington pecking order assured that he and Sarah were often invited to White House social events, this was the first time Melanie was included, and it was the first time he felt that he was an intimate part of the occasion rather than an obligatory invite from the "A" list. He felt like the father of the bride. He had taken Sally into his heart, and he felt enriched by her happiness.

As for Sally and Griff, the road had been winding and fraught with bumps and bruises, but they were together now and mature enough to appreciate what they had in each other. Two amazing life events at once! A Cinderella wedding in the White House and a new life growing and stirring in Sally's belly! Sally, the small town girl from Iowa, had come a very long way from her beginnings, and Griff, whose detours had almost done him in, had made the long walk as well. They were perfect together.

Chapter 53

For the next week, Sabir and his Israeli buddies worked their cell phones. With Griff's help, a plan evolved to send Nayif to Israel under the protection of Sabir's friends where the water technology experts at Technion would train him. In the meantime, Amos would set up King Khalid for Nayif's return. To replace the Nighthawks, the President proposed to the King that Griff prepare an economic package, that he had some ideas on some of the elements it might contain and that these ideas included an environmental component to support Amos' environmental initiative. He didn't mention the specifics of their plan. They needed a little more time to flesh out the pieces and prepare Nayif to spearhead the effort, but the basics were beginning to fall into place. At this point, the King didn't seem to care too much about the details. He was desperate for the money.

ICE cooperated with their Israeli compatriots and arranged for Li to speak to Sabir who assured her she would be okay. Arrangements were made to have her deported to a specific destination in Hong Kong where they would meet. Later, Sabir would learn that Li was more resourceful than he had imagined. While she was tending Sally, she removed two diamonds from their chains and one from her ring, and skillfully sewed them into the soft padding of her bra. Each flawless diamond weighed at least 10 carats and each was valued at more than $300,000. Li was harboring about a million dollars close to her heart.

Escorted by an ICE agent, Li was flown to New York where they both boarded a China Southern flight to Hong Kong with a short stopover in San Francisco. After they arrived at Hong Kong International Airport, the agent escorted Li to the front desk of the Regal Airport Hotel where there were prepaid reservations in her name for the Nirvana

Suite, and he left. Li was completely on her own for the first time in her life, no parents to watch over her, no madam to manage her time, no appointments to keep, no girls to take care of, no Amir to watch her movements, no prison cell to bar her from life's possibilities. She was a free agent now and the choices she made from this day forward would be made because she chose to make them and for no other reason. The air she breathed felt lighter now.

A hotel captain was assigned to Li and led her to the suite. Li gasped when the door was opened. It was a sleek all-white contemporary space with natural light flooding every corner. Concealing a huge Jacuzzi tub, there was a glass block divider that was lit from within and glowed with the fire of a thousand candles. The fragrance of jasmine pervaded the room and fine champagne and an enticing iced bowl of Beluga caviar sat on the cocktail table. There were huge bowls of fresh flowers dressing the sitting area, fruits and herbal teas on the bar, a soft white chenille robe flung across the bed, and a variety of oils and body scrubs on the bathtub ledge. The thought crossed Li's mind that she had traveled a very long way from the Putuo slums because she felt completely at ease in these luxurious surroundings.

After being assured that everything met with her approval, the captain handed a sealed envelope to Li and left. She sprawled on a lounge chair, and opened it.

My Dearest Li,

When you receive this letter you will be safely ensconced at the Regal, and I will be counting the days until I see you again. There is a bank account in your name at the Hong Kong and Shanghai Bank and an envelope with cash in a safe deposit box, which you can access at the front desk of the hotel.

Li, I owe you so much, but I want you to know that the only thing you owe me is your happiness. You awakened my senses to the joys of love and to the colors and fragrances of the earth. If your heart is open to the love my heart holds for you, it is yours for as long as you want it. We shall speak of this when I see you on the new moon.

Meanwhile, ask for Soo Yung at Noble House Custom Tailors and have an elegant wardrobe made of the finest fabrics she has to offer. She is expecting you and understands what I have in mind.

Until we are together, you give meaning to my thoughts and dreams.

Sabir

Li was not expecting Sabir's declaration of love, but she was not surprised by it either. She had a little more than a week before Sabir arrived, time to examine her life and see if she could cleanse it of the past and recharge it for the future. She wasn't sure how it would turn out, but she was eager to find out. Sabir was a very special man.

Chapter 54

There were some rumblings that the Saudis were working on a deal with the Administration, and Mahmood Zandipour was irritated because he knew nothing about it. Still fairly new to the scene, he lacked a network of close contacts and with Nayif out of the picture; he had few avenues to pursue for good information. Through his embassy, President Zahedi was demanding answers, and he had none. Mahmood had nightmares of his head on a chopping block, and he was not far off the mark.

Iran had chosen the path of isolation when she had forged ahead with her nuclear weapons program even as the international community joined together to try to dissuade her. Back then, she was rolling in oil money and her visions of Persian Gulf and even world domination seemed within reach. Now, with little demand for oil and with petro-dollars slowed to a trickle, she was mired in debt and shunned by her Gulf neighbors and the Western powers.

The Saudis were looking out for themselves. Iran had only Russia and China to turn to, but they had serious problems of their own and she could offer them no incentives of any value to entice them to come to her rescue.

Time and again, through a variety of regional and international bodies, Iran had been offered inclusion in the discussion of regional security issues, a generous trade and cooperation agreement, other economic incentives, technical advice on just about everything, and full access to nuclear fuel more appropriate to the peaceful generation of nuclear power. In return, Iran had to cease enriching uranium for the production of nuclear weapons and allow regular inspections of its nuclear facilities. The choice some said was between "jobs and bombs."

Iran chose bombs. As a result, the United States and Israel entered into a security pact that resulted in the emplacement of a successfully tested missile shield. A united international community finally reacted to the danger of a nuclear-armed Iran and imposed tough-minded and vigorously enforced sanctions. China's young leadership decided the time was right to spread its influence beyond the Pacific Rim. They had built a huge navy and flexed their emerging muscle with the dispatch of a carrier group to the Persian Gulf to join a U.S. 5th fleet that now welcomed their partnership. As a result of this convergence of power, Iran was increasingly isolated from the rest of the world, both economically and politically. Jobs were scarce, universities and hospitals were closing, potholes were proliferating, garbage was left in the streets, shops were boarded up, government employees were on a three-day workweek, military personnel were unpaid, and unrest was stirring throughout the land.

It seemed that the Iranian ideological thrust for a new Golden Age of Islamic domination uber alles was drawing to a close. Even the Iranian rulers were beginning to understand this, especially when King Khalid would not take President Zahedi's calls, nor would he respond to his frantic messages.

Amos viewed Iran's worsening plight as an opening. He and Griff met to update the parameters of the languishing economic package and to go over the increased demands they wanted to make for its implementation. Amos consulted with other world leaders and sought their advice and their participation. All agreed it was dangerous to have loose nukes floating around in a failed state and that the time was probably ripe to squeeze Iran into submission. They also agreed that it was important to treat them with dignity, especially when they had them pinned to the floor.

The planning would be kept under the radar until it was ready. In the meantime, Amos would stay in touch with Zahedi, hold his hand, listen to his problems, and hold out promise that they would soon be solved.

Fully briefed on the progress of the water technology plan, Amos believed he could depend on Griff and Nayif to move the Saudi initiative forward. Iran was the last intractable piece in the Middle East dilemma, but for the first time, Amos saw a glimmer of light at the end of the tunnel.

Chapter 55

Sally was back at the wheel. One of the three thugs who had grabbed her was arrested on a drug charge. In short order, he brought up the kidnapping caper and fingered the other two culprits so he could get his drug charge reduced to a misdemeanor. That left only the enigmatic Amir still unaccounted for. Although the search for him continued, with Sally safe there was less urgency and the file was activated only on slow days. It was abundantly clear to the authorities which bad guys were behind the kidnapping, but with Griff and Amos concurring, the Saudi and the Iranian governments were let off the hook. No doubt they would be more pliable now and in the long term that would serve a larger purpose.

For Sally, life at the Foster place was a perfect fit for her schedule. She and Griff worked hard and sometimes attended work related events in the evening. Coming home to a turned-down bed, fresh towels, clean laundry and a good dinner, suited them just fine. For Arthur and Pamela Foster, the house was more alive than it had been for ages, and they loved every minute of it. They cajoled their part-time staff to work more days, and on Thursdays, the cook's day off, they turned out amazing food specialties that were ready and waiting for the newlyweds whenever they showed up.

The Fosters made a proposal to Griff and Sally that was too hard to refuse. They would renovate the second floor for them, which was large enough to accommodate a nursery, a nanny's room, a master bedroom suite with a comfortable sitting room, and a kitchenette. The Fosters would move their master suite up to the third floor, which offered more than enough space for them, and they would have full use of the lift. Sally and Griff needed all of two seconds to consider the plan. It solved all of their worries about giving the baby full time care while keeping their busy jobs. They would hire a nanny but with the Fosters around, they would feel more comfortable leaving the baby in the nanny's care. With a nice raise in her pocket, Sophie wanted to move from her cramped apartment to a house, and Sally's place fit the bill. Sally sold the place to Sophie at the appraisal price, well below the market price, which made it an easy transaction. Sally made a profit, Sophie got a deal, and everyone was satisfied.

The Fosters, who were realistic about their advancing years, put the Georgetown house in an irrevocable trust for Sally and Griff, which removed it from their considerable estate, and they celebrated the agreement with a gourmet dinner at the Club and an exchange of gifts.

For Sally and Griff, the golden couple on every Washington "A" list, life was good, and with a baby on the way, it could only get better. The rough patches they had both struggled with along the way were becoming vague memories that seemed to belong to strangers.

Chapter 56

Through a series of wireless communications and videoconferences, both mid-level and high-level, King Khalid understood that the Nighthawks were a lost cause, and in any case he realized that military jets were not a solution to his mounting economic problems. There was only one realistic way forward to assure his financial well-being. He would have to bring the cousins to consensus and name Nayif as the new Crown Prince. No use chasing Sabir around the globe to a dead end! He had had enough of dead ends. At long last, he accepted the unalterable fact that the ground had shifted beneath him, and if he didn't want to be sucked into its crevices, he needed to change course. Nayif gave him a way out, and it was clear that Amos Jackson was in Nayif's corner. It was emotionally difficult for him to come to this conclusion but no matter what other flaws he possessed, when it came to money he was no fool. The King responded to Sabir's latest overture, and they made their peace. Despite their differences, a strong childhood bond and a memory bank of pleasant times helped to bridge them. Nayif was the new Crown Prince, and Sabir was now the free man he wished to be.

Several months earlier, CIA agents had delivered Nayif from the Foster place in Georgetown to the Israeli Embassy on International Drive near Rock Creek Park. Well protected by Israeli agents, Nayif was flown to Tel Aviv and driven to the Negev kibbutz to join his father. There, Nayif was briefed on his new role and after shaking off the inevitable jet lag, he began to understand the significance of it. Could he do this? He trembled with anxiety, but he was also buoyed by the possibilities of a meaningful life. Still, his heart told him that before he could move on he had to make his peace with Allah.

At last alone in the small sleeping room assigned to him, he observed the setting sun and turned toward Mecca. With profound humility and a terrible fear that Allah knew of his mortal sins, he dropped to his wobbly knees. As he was taught, he breathed deeply and tried to purge his mind of worrisome thoughts so he could focus his thoughts toward the heavens.

"Allah hu Akbar.

Allah hu Akbar.

God is great

God is great

Ash-hadu an la,

Ila ha-illallah.

I bear witness there is no God but God."

"Allah, the most merciful and compassionate, I ask your forgiveness for my mortal sins, and I ask your guidance in the path I have been chosen to follow. With your help, merciful Allah, I pledge to you that I shall walk this path with honor and humility until the end of my days on earth. Inshallah."

Twists and turns had brought Nayif to this place. His future was set. Like a rolling stone gathering bittersweet moss along the way, he had finally come to his fated place in the road.

Sabir needed assurances of protection from Joshua before he could simply leave Nayif to fend for himself in a strange land. General Joshua Peretz rose to the occasion and offered to look after him. Peretz, a family man with three grown children and a grandchild on the way, lived in

Haifa's affluent upper city of Mount Carmel with his wife Alana. Nayif would live with them while he trained at Technion, which was located very close by. In Haifa, a beautiful city overlooking a broad bay, Jews and Arabs lived and worked side by side in peaceful and friendly co-existence and Peretz believed Nayif would feel comfortable in this place. He would see to it.

The General, an influential member of the Knesset, was a man who had spent his life trying to build bridges of brotherhood. He was born and raised in this place, a city that was a center of the B'hai faith, a faith that taught the unity of all religions and claimed the equal divinity of all of the prophets. The General explained to Sabir that the B'hais believed that each prophet, whether Abraham, Moses, Buddha, Krishna, Jesus, Muhammad, or Baha'ullah, was sent at a different time to convey holy messages that were relevant to his particular era. This made some sense to the General.

General Joshua Peretz, a secular Jew who had studied both the classics and the teachings of Torah, believed that strict religious practices did not always square with his view of civilized human behavior. Nothing upset him more than the rigid religious divides that sometimes festered among his own people. Nothing puzzled him more than the intolerance that all faiths too often felt for one another. Nothing saddened him more than the awful times when he was called to arms to quell flare-ups between Palestinians and Jews, and nothing pleased him more than the hopeful peace that had finally come.

Although there was still the occasional uprising, a sporatic eruption of old grievances, by and large, on both sides of the boundary lines, everyone was working, everyone was eating well, everyone was drinking clean water, everyone lived in decent housing, everyone had access to education and health care, and most peace-loving citizens were satisfied with the outcome of the tough negotiations that had produced the final map of the two-state solution. The building blocks for a nonviolent Middle East were coming together, but a few more pieces needed to fall into place before the end game could be reached.

Nayif did not know this yet, but he would return to his native land not only with the technical knowledge to make the desert bloom and the cash to make it possible, but also with a dream of peace and brotherhood securely locked away in his heart.

On the new moon, Sabir flew to Hong Kong to begin an extraordinary chapter of his already extraordinary life.

Chapter 57

Another summer whispered its hesitant goodbye. At Laurelwood, lonely fall leaves lingered on the nearly naked branches of the trees that seemed reluctant to shed them. For Griff, and for Celeste and Charles, the painful memories of Winn's violent end were receding into the shadows and kinder recollections of a more distant past were winning the struggle to replace them. Life, as it often does, was overcoming sorrow and good memories were creeping into the heart to suffocate the unbearable ones.

Celeste, with Charles at her side, had found happiness and contentment. Because of Charles she was spared the necessity of learning to live alone, and in Charles she found a treasure beyond her imaginings. Her empty heart had been waiting and Winn's tragic death paved the way for Charles to fill it. These days, she and Charles were comfortable arriving together to place Laurelwood flowers on Winn's grave and when Celeste reached out to Winn to speak to him of her new life, she believed that he heard her message and was happy for her.

As for Griff, he had filled his life after Winn with a love he could not have conjured in his wildest dreams and with a new job that gave him a chance to move mountains. As if all of this was not enough he was about to climb to an even higher pinnacle of happiness. Sally and he eagerly awaited the birth of their baby. For both of these weathered souls, this baby was an extraordinary gift from God; His way of promising that little pieces of each of them would survive long after they were gone.

After Sally's rescue they had begun to attend church on Sunday mornings and in the sway of prayer their minds were somehow opened to miracles. The lessons of their Christian faith were slowly triumphing over an earlier skepticism and a power beyond them found a dwelling place within them. For Sally, with past hurts over and done and new life coming, prayer became the pathway for thoughts of gratitude; and for Griff, prayer became the guiding hand that relieved his daily personal struggle with a demon that would never wholly disappear. Although their inquiring minds never ceased to question, they struggled through the dry spells and hung on to their newfound faith.

Now, they were in a place in their lives that was filled with the thrill of anticipation. To make it all seem more real, Sally and Griff pored over baby names on the Web and selected the name Theodora, from the Greek "gift from God." They would call her Teddy, which seemed like a nice cuddly name for a little girl.

The nursery was ready. The Afghan was done. The doctor had scheduled the Caesarian section. The "girls" were marking off the remaining days on the calendar. Sally's bag was packed. All that was left to do was to bring Teddy into the world.

Everything went without a hitch. Teddy, having been spared the traumatic journey through the birth canal, was gently lifted out without a mark on her. She was pink, and soft, and beautiful with just a little bit of blonde fuzz on her nearly baldhead. Her little fingers were curled tight into tiny fists, her pudgy toes were wiggling and her sweet small voice was crying quietly, as if she didn't want to disturb her drowsy mother. Griff could not hold back his tears. They were tears of wonder, tears of joy and tears of relief that Sally was fine and Teddy was perfect. From the first moment that he held her in his arms and felt her heart beat, a fresh chamber of his own heart was opened and for the rest of his life that chamber overflowed with a special love that belonged only to Teddy.

When Sally emerged from her foggy state, Griff gently placed Teddy into her arms. Sally's smiling face was glowing with a new kind of happiness, a look of utter contentment and joy, and she said, "She looks like an angel, doesn't she, Griff? She feels so soft. Look at her dainty little fingers, so perfect. We have to keep her safe, Griff. We will just love her and keep her safe," and with that Sally fell fast asleep, the smile still on her lips.

The private lounge was awash in people — Charles and Celeste, Betsy and her Secret Service agents, the Fosters, Feld and Sarah, Sophie, Raj and even Jimmy Wu. Amos, who realized he would create too much of a stir if he came, was kept abreast of the action by an excited and breathless Betsy. He could not help but think about the tacit pact of silence that had permeated all the childless years that had torn at his heart and Betsy's, and he hoped they would be the Godparents. No baby was ever more wanted than Teddy.

Chapter 58

Sabir arrived on the new moon to a place that offered great promise for a life very different from the one he had left behind. Li waited for him in the hotel lobby and hoped that her heart would race when he walked through the door. She was dressed in a custom tailored, cream-colored silk brocade suit with three carved ivory buttons and a very slim skirt that needed long side slits for movement. It had been expertly hand stitched by Soo Yung of the finest fabrics Hong Kong had to offer. Li's flawless face was gently highlighted with a touch of cheek color and lip-gloss. It was attractively framed by her ebony hair, which was gathered into a French twist that was secured by two amber hair sticks. The only jewelry she wore was a huge round cut diamond ring sitting high on her index finger. Exquisite by any standards, the men and even the women who were passing through the lobby could not resist a second look.

Sabir arrived, Li's heart raced, and their future was sealed. After spending a few days together renewing their old feelings and getting used to the fresh ones that their newfound freedom allowed them to explore, they talked about the practical aspects of their life together. Sabir had money to burn, but he needed to be in a place where there would be no restrictions on the amount he could bring in and no impediments to investing it. Macau, on the other side of the long Hong Kong-Macau Bridge, which had opened in 2020, was such a place. It was also a place that welcomed expatriates, a special region with a high degree of autonomy that operated under China's "one country – two systems" policy, a place where he would feel as welcome as Li.

While the sun was setting in the West on the great Las Vegas boom, the sun was rising in the East over the islands of Macau. With the bridge complete and a transportation network in place, Chinese and international investors were flocking to Macau to build world-class luxury condos, 6 star hotels and huge casinos. Casino managers from Vegas were settling in with their families. Tourism was exploding, especially from the Mainland, and neighborhoods of mansions and high-rise condos were springing up all over the place, scarfing up all the scarce land they could find on these two small islands. There was even a small mosque for a thousand or so of Sabir's brethren who had discovered Macau before he had.

The Cotai Strip, a re-creation of the Vegas strip, was expected to drive Macau into the major leagues, and it was here that Sabir and Li laid down their marker. They would help transform Macau into an Asian resort destination with more to offer than gambling. It was here that Sabir and Li developed their own six star hotel, which Li, to the end of her days, watched over in the minutest detail. It was here that Sabir put together a successful financial empire that was fueled mainly by the search for high yield investments by his wealthy Arab brothers of the Persian Gulf.

For Sabir and Li, the Cotai Strip became a street of dreams, and their Putuo Resort Hotel, where they were ensconced in its elegant penthouse tower, a reminder that it doesn't matter much how your life begins but it matters a great deal how you play the cards you are dealt. Until the day he died of old age, Sabir was intoxicated by Li's beauty, and Li never got enough of Sabir's kind heart, his keen intellect, his tender touch, and even his harmless peccadillos. They had each led many lives but the last was by far the best.

Chapter 59

Nayif learned his lessons well. Sabir paved the way, and the new Crown Prince was welcomed to Jeddah like a conquering hero. Once again he was escorted to the King's Palace, but this time he felt no disquiet at all. This time his heart fluttered in excitement but not in fear. When he crossed the threshold of the arched granite entry, he walked with humility in his heart but with his head and shoulders high, for someday this palace would be his home.

They had laid a long red carpet for him. The King's honor guards had donned their red dress uniforms with epaulets and gold cords draped on the shoulders, and they stood at attention on each side of the carpet to salute him. The King was waiting for him in the Inner Courtyard, but times had changed. This time, His Royal Highness rose from his chair and came forward to meet him. After the obligatory greetings, the King took Nayif's hand in his and guided him to a bench overlooking the Red Sea. He sat and motioned for Nayif to sit beside him.

"My dear nephew," said the King, "You return to this Courtyard bearing gifts to save the Kingdom, and for this I am most grateful. I am an old man and I am a stubborn one. The habits of a lifetime are ingrained in me. My headstrong ways have not helped our people, and I am wise enough to know that I must relinquish them and give you free reign if you are to accomplish your tasks. So let it be, Crown Prince Nayif. With Allah's blessing and with the help of your friends in Israel and America, you shall make our desert bloom, and you shall save our people from financial ruin."

"The waters of the Red Sea that we gaze upon from this place have bathed and fed the multitudes of our ancestors. These are the very same waters that yielded to the will of God when they swallowed the

Pharaoh's armies and saved the fleeing Israelites. If the descendants of those Israelites can save us in our hour of need, God must have His hand in it."

"Allah be praised, perhaps the time has come for the sons of Abraham to forgive one another. Just as Ishmael's mother Hagar found water for him when he was near dead from thirst, you shall find water and give life to the desert sands when we are near dead from a different thirst. As Hagar said, 'If it is God's will, let what God's will be done.'"

"Allah hu Akbar"

"Allah hu Akbar."

"Aiaisha awaits your return, and her people have arranged your marriage. She is a lovely girl and still young, and I shall pray to Allah to bless you with many heirs. The family must continue to be strong in number. Inshallah."

Nayif quickly set to work. With Griff's financial and administrative support and Technion's technical support, he brought in instructors, engineers, technicians, workers and managers. They came in large numbers on American and Israeli passports that were welcomed with only token inspection. Jews for the first time in centuries recited their own prayers on the same Arabian soil that at least three tribes of their ancient ancestors had called home. The ill-conceived era of Saudiization, when skilled foreign workers were ejected to make way for Saudis, had come to an end.

With Nayif at the helm, an encampment was established that was sensitive to the separate religious needs of each group. Saudi nationals now worked side by side with foreigners from other lands who were no longer pariahs in their land. The Saudis quickly learned all they were taught, and with newly honed skills they put their heads together with foreign experts to overcome the unique problems of this vast and forbidding desert. With modifications, the Israeli water carrier system was replicated with a modern network of pipelines, canals, reservoirs and tunnels. Roads were built and towns promptly cropped up along the way. With backbreaking but satisfying work, seeds were planted in the furrows, sprinklers were installed to water the newly planted earth, and greenhouses were built to border the roads like rows of soldiers standing in line as far as the eye could see. Here in this desert, an oasis sprung up to bury the Arabian sands and give its inhabitants a foretaste of Paradise.

From dawn to dusk the work continued and the men who wiped their brows together came to know one another. Their religious differences paled as they shared their hopes and dreams and spoke as one of the loneliness they suffered away from their homes and their families. Above all, they shared great joy when the fruits of their hard labor turned green and burst through the newly fertile soil. Nayif, imbued with the spirit of unity he had learned in Haifa, walked among the workers, shared a meal with them, learned to fix a sprinkler head and repair a greenhouse panel, shared pictures of Aiaisha and of his children, and was admired and accepted as one of them.

Over the years, Amos and Griff made sure that Nayif had all the expertise and the money that he needed to complete the project. Even after the White House years were over, Amos kept his hand in it, and Griff continued to participate in the Conference. At their behest, the Israelis and the Americans co-funded the King Khalid Institute of Technology in Riyadh, and professors from Technion and MIT came to get it off the ground. Nayif became a highly respected lecturer at Technion and at each Global Environmental Initiative Conference.

Nayif had walked many pathways and each pathway brought him closer to the great man he would become. The humility that became a deep-rooted part of his nature would someday make him a beloved King.

Chapter 60

The Iranian economic package was ready. Mahmood Zandipour was the go-between, and he worked for almost two years with Griff's staff to get as much as he could in desperately needed cash and in goods and services. In return, there was a tough trade agreement that guaranteed access through the narrow and strategic Straits of Hormuz, and an international security agreement that would immediately secure and dismantle the nukes with a robust verification regime to assure their nonexistence. The Israelis had attempted to destroy those weapons on more than one occasion, but the facilities were scattered and deep and the Israeli bunker busters met with only limited success.

Griff and Amos both understood the importance of supporting Zahedi's tiresome but congenital need to save face. On every principal issue, Amos initiated a call to him and had a charming way of getting Zahedi to believe the ideas were his own. Since the pompous President of this ancient civilization viewed himself with overblown self-importance and believed he was the true world leader, this was a critical element in reaching a winning conclusion.

However, the fates intervened before the agreement was signed. Once again, the people of Iran had had enough, and they rebelled. But this time, the Revolutionary Guards and their well-armed militias crossed the Rubicon and stood shoulder to shoulder with their fellow citizens. They rose up together and Zahedi was lucky to escape their wrath with his life. He fled the country for parts unknown and although rumors of his whereabouts would abound, he was never heard from again.

The people were in charge now, cultured people descended from givers of law, founders of medicine, devotees of art and poetry, and from among them, wise leaders emerged who kept the uprising from spinning out of control. Many former leaders, long disillusioned by Zahedi and his henchmen's well-known support of terrorism, stepped up to the plate and eagerly joined the new ones. With the streets calmed and the people united, competitive and monitored elections were scheduled under Iran's democratic constitution that would at last be free and fair.

Iran's ruling Ayatollahs were left with little choice. They were obliged to recognize that their harsh and centralized interpretation of sharia law no longer had a place in a democratic society of educated people whose world included the Web. At long last, these rigid theocrats realized that their implicit and explicit support and export of radicalism was counterproductive to their own survival. They accepted that to retain any power at all, they would have to separate their views and actions from civil authority and allow the government to be answerable directly to the ordinary citizens who elected them, everyday people who lived their lives here on earth.

Privately, Amos and Griff rejoiced. This was better than they could have hoped for, but they had no choice but to wait it out. They worked the phones, kept in touch with the relevant players, but realized they had to steer clear of tilting one way or another until the elections were held.

Mahmood was not recalled. He was considered a placeholder and no one paid much attention to him. With hours to kill, he searched the Web for news accounts that explored the history and current actions of his people, had time to reflect on his angry point of view and grew to be a more mellow man.

The elections were held. Muhammad Ali Bokhtar, a leader of the uprising, was elected President by an overwhelming majority of the people. Amos called to congratulate him, and he was invited by

President-Elect Bokhtar to attend his inauguration ceremony and the festivities to follow.

The new Iranian foreign minister concluded arrangements for the economic and security agreements, which were scheduled for signature two months after the inauguration. The signing would occur during Ali Bokhtar's first official visit to Washington. Iran did not want to appear to be in a financial crisis, nor did it want to highlight the nukes issue. In an amicable manner, it was agreed by all the parties that there be no fanfare and the signing was handled as regular business.

The nuclear weapons were dismantled; the world was a safer place; the citizens of Iran had triumphed and the free world had a vibrant new participant.

On the most difficult of issues, Amos and Griff had done a masterful job. They toasted one another, Amos with fine wine; Griff with ginger ale. For each of them, there was the rich taste of victory in every sip.

Chapter 61

As blessings go, Teddy was of the highest order. From the first, she was a placid baby who rarely cried and spent most of her time sleeping, gurgling or gazing at the clucking faces around her. By the time she was three months old, she had dimples in her elbows and cheeks, sharpei puppy dog folds on her thighs, and a perpetual smile on her rosebud lips. Right from the start, she was passed from one set of loving arms to another, and without hesitation, she eagerly went to everyone with outstretched arms. One tiny baby girl gave so much joy to the hearts of so many different people; it was a wondrous thing that each could say this was the best of times.

Instinctively, Griff and Sally knew that Amos and Betsy ached to be the godparents. Griff discussed this with Celeste who assured him she would feel just as honored to be a favorite aunt but it would make her very happy if Teddy would wear her heirloom-christening gown at the baptism. Betsy and Amos already adored Teddy and, needless to say, the privilege of being selected as godparents meant a great deal to them. Their positions were more isolating than most people realized, and although they knew a slew of people who claimed them as close friends, they were cautious and counted only a few as theirs.

To prepare for the big day, which was to be on All Saint's Day, the first Sunday after the first of November, Betsy had some private sessions on Baptism with the Rector at St. Johns Episcopal Church and shared her lessons with Celeste during their usual gabfests. Celeste retrieved her christening gown from an attic trunk, and she and Betsy went over it with a fine toothcomb to make sure it was perfect. It was not only perfect; it was exquisite. The dress was a frothy concoction of pretty whitework floral designs with fine pin-tucking and masses of

Valencienne lace, and Celeste reminisced that her mother had said it was all put together entirely by hand. Celeste also dug out her christening bonnet, which had alternating rows of similar flowers with two layers of lace around the crown and in the front. Teddy was going to look like a little princess at her christening.

The christening took place in November, and Teddy slept through the event except for the few seconds when she was disturbed by the sprinkle of holy water. Even then, she only whimpered slightly and turned her head away. It was a touching ceremony, with Amos and Betsy vowing to keep Teddy away from the worldly temptations of greed, malice and selfishness, and to teach her the ways by which she could be drawn closer to God. They recited the words; "She is now ours to raise in this faith, ours to teach, ours to love, ours to protect, ours to cherish, and ours to walk with."

Griff and Sally beamed at the astonishing turn their lives had taken, and at long last, Godparents Betsy and Amos had a child to love. This kind of happiness doesn't happen only in fairy tales. It happens to hearts that are open to it.

Celeste and Charles were also leading incredibly happy lives. They had each other. They had their gardens. They had a pleasant social life with a few close and caring friends, and now they had Teddy. When she was little, try as they may not to be excessive they could not keep from showering her with presents, keeping her favorite home baked cookies on a low shelf in the pantry where she could reach them, taking her to her favorite places like the Washington Zoo to visit the pandas or on special treks to Rockefeller Center in New York at Christmas to see the big Christmas tree.

To the good fortune of Teddy's extended family, Griff and Sally were happy to share her. Both of them were still deeply committed to their work, and this arrangement seemed just right for them and for Teddy.

Amos and Betsy not only took Teddy into their hearts, but they also took seriously their responsibilities as godparents. When they were still in the White House and their lives were overcrowded with full schedules and the constant demands of an insatiable public, they still found private time for sleepovers for Teddy. When Teddy came, carrying her pink Little Miss Kitty weekend bag and one of her dozens of Teddy bears dangling on her arm, everyone smiled. She had free reign to sit in on any meeting, crawl under any table, skip down any hall, sleep in any bed she chose, or munch on any cookie on the cookie trays purposely put out for her in her favorite places and, on nice days, she was allowed to run around the White House lawn to bounce balls, skip rope and climb trees. On these visits Betsy spent every spare minute with her, and Amos joined them whenever he could. At bedtime, wherever Teddy chose to sleep, Betsy read to her from Bible Stories for Little Children, and Amos taught her the same parables his father had taught him.

As for the Fosters, they found excuses to skip their annual winter holiday to their villa in the south of France and avoided long cruises altogether. They felt so lucky to finally have a grandchild and especially lucky that she lived under the same roof with them. Griff had been raised mostly by nannies while they were busy making official rounds on a demanding Washington party circuit, and they had missed out on so much of his childhood. Although they still enjoyed their old friends and an occasional party, nothing gave them the kind of high that Teddy did. She was their second chance, and they simply couldn't get enough of her.

Occasionally, the Felds invited the "group" for a Friday Sabbath dinner — ten or twelve gathered around the table depending upon whether Amos and Betsy could make it. Sally and Griff, Amos and Betsy, Celeste and Charles, Pamela and Arthur, Sarah, Feld and Melanie, and Teddy who was like a central force, a little angel holding them all together. On those Fridays, there was a traditional Sabbath dinner – matzo ball soup, roast stuffed chicken or duck, and especially for Amos, Sarah's delicious homemade lemon meringue pie. The candle lighting was Teddy's favorite thing. Sarah, wearing her perpetual smile, covered her head with a kerchief, lit the Sabbath candles with care, then cupped her hands over her eyes and chanted the ancient Hebrew blessing. As the golden glow of candlelight cast radiance on the faces around the table, Sarah recited a Sabbath poem that had been passed down to her through the generations of her ancestors:

My Mother's Sabbath candles
Made our loving home so bright.
So carefully she lit the flame,
With a prayer each Friday night.
And then around the table,
We gathered and we heard,
My father chant the Kiddush,
His heart in every word.
All the tragic stories
Of Israel's darkest night
Never dimmed the glory
Of my mother's Sabbath light.

Then, Feld recited the Kiddush, the blessing for the kosher wine, and everyone took a sip, including Teddy and Griff who were both served grape juice. Last, Feld chanted the blessing for bread over the braided Challah in Hebrew, and everyone, including Teddy, sang the prayer in English. In keeping with Jewish tradition, the Challah was passed, and each person tore a piece of bread and ate it. It was then that Teddy knew the ceremony was over, and she clapped her hands in delight and just kept right on singing.

One would think all of the attention lavished upon Teddy would spoil her. But it was impossible to alter the innate goodness and gentle nature that came in the package called Teddy. This special child aptly named Theodora, a gift from God, was the realization of the dreams and the yearnings of so many people, and thankfully, she was born with more than enough love to go around.

Chapter 62

Soon after Teddy was born, Sally phoned Melba to tell her. Melba sounded genuinely happy, and asked Sally to send photos of Teddy along with her Mother's Day card, that is, if it wasn't too much trouble. She said she would also appreciate a wedding photo of Griff and Sally, if she had one to spare. The routine, two phone calls a year were usually short and to the point, but this one took a little longer. Sally who was now back in harness almost full throttle, made a mental note to send the photos and stay in touch.

Teddy was nearly four, and with Amos two years into his final term, Griff was busy prodding AID's environmental project bosses to keep moving ahead at a steady pace. His goal was to have enough visually ready for Amos so he could make a grand tour in the next year or two. Griff and his entourage would visit the sites now, check on their progress first hand, establish some priorities for the next years, scope out the good visuals, and identify the key players who would host Amos on his tour. Griff's trip would take at least a month. Sally was excited for him and suggested she assign a foreign correspondent and a camera crew to go along and do a series that would serve as a set-up piece for the later trip.

Sally was telephoning her mother more frequently now, and said, "You know, Griff, since you're going to be gone for so long, it might be a great opportunity for me to take a time out and introduce Teddy to my mother. It's been forever since I've seen her, and she has become a loose end that I feel a strong need to tie. I know so little about her, so little about both of my parents, so little about my own childhood! I never gave it a thought until Teddy, but now there are times when I can't get these thoughts out of my mind. Then again, maybe I should just leave it alone!"

Griff looked at Sally long and hard, and replied, "Until you see her and learn more about her and yourself, seems to me you may leave a piece of you that always feels unfinished, an empty place that gnaws at you, that begs to be filled. You have to decide for yourself, Sally, but the visit sounds like a good idea to me." Griff held out his arms, and Sally nestled in the familiar crook of his neck, in the spot where she could take in the sensual fragrance of his freshly washed hair and inhale the inviting scent of his English bath soap. Even though they stood shoulder to shoulder, when he put his arms around her she felt so little, so sheltered and safe, she liked to nestle there for a while. Griff understood her need, and he never pulled away until she was ready to let go.

"That settles it, Griff. Teddy and I are going to make that trip!"

When Griff's departure date was set, Sally made arrangements to fly out of Washington to Iowa City and rent a car there for the 35 mile drive to her mother's home in Columbus Junction, Iowa. She could barely remember the town, which stretched two miles in either direction from Highway 92 with a population of 2000 people scattered along the way. It was a place where there was some of the best soil in the world, but people mostly scraped out a meager living. Sometimes Mother Nature threw them curveballs that made a hard life even harder, but small town mid-westerners are a resilient people, and they just kept bouncing back. Sally drove slowly past hog farms, and corn and soybean fields, a beef processing plant and a bio-fuels facility, all not very far from the Columbus Community High School where she had gotten her start on the school paper.

With Teddy safely snuggled in her car seat fast asleep, Sally took a detour and drove past the public library on Maple Street where she had spent so much of her spare time, past the United Methodist Church on 2nd Street that had served as a Sunday haven for her early days, and ended up driving the length of the Louisa County Fairgrounds, which she knew would be barren until July came around. She realized that she was a little nervous, probably stalling the moment of reunion, and she finally turned towards her mother's house on Oak Street. It was not the house she had grown up in but the house that was built to replace it after the Great Iowa River Flood of 2029.

Melba had told her that everyone in town put up a good fight sandbagging the banks, but the river burst through the three levees that held back the floodwaters, and the swollen river finally won the fight. Melba's home was washed away, and the town folk pulled together to build her a new one. Sally passed the Four Corners Restaurant and wondered if Melba still waitressed there. Suddenly, she realized that her conversations with her mother were one-sided, mainly about Sally, and then Teddy and very little about her mother. Sally turned into the dirt driveway of 134 Oak Street, pulled up behind an aging but freshly washed sedan and parked.

Melba opened the front door and came across the porch and down the few steps at breakneck speed. Suddenly she hesitated as if she were unsure of how to greet her daughter. Sally made it easy. She took a few steps towards her and opened her arms. Melba, overcome with emotion, hugged Sally tight and burst into tears. She wiped them away with the back of her hand, helped Sally lift Teddy out of the car seat, and she carried her into the house. Sally came behind them with a large duffle, a small Little Miss Kitty weekend bag and a Teddy bear. Then both of them spoke at the same time. "It's been so long!" Then Sally said, "It's good to see you, Mom." Melba replied in kind. "It's good to see you, too Sally. Can I get you anything? A coke? Some water?"

"No, let's just sit a while. See if we can make enough noise to wake up Miss Sleepyhead. She's been up since 5 o'clock this morning, and I think she's probably exhausted. The house looks good, Mom. It looks like the old one except for whiter paint and newer furniture. If you like, we can leave Teddy on the sofa while you show me around."

Melba took Sally's hand and led her into the dining room. Sally caught her breath for there on the buffet and on the dining room table sat every Mother's Day card and birthday card Sally had ever sent, all opened and sitting upright. Mingled among them, in neat matching silver frames were Sally and Griff's wedding photograph, and every photograph of Teddy that Sally had mailed to her.

"I couldn't save much from the floodwaters, but thank goodness I had time to save my most precious possessions, these cards and photographs, my marriage certificate and a photograph of your father. There just wasn't time to gather anything else."

Now, it was Sally's turn to cry. And cry she did. All the pent-up emotion, all the guilt, all her confused feelings spilled out in enough floodwater to rival the river's. She and Melba stood there, both crying, and held on to each other while the years of separation just faded away. Now they were two adults who could embark together on a journey of understanding.

Teddy was still fast asleep, and they continued the tour. The house was nice, everything neat and clean with little touches of flowers, curtains, and pretty prints and paintings hanging in the right places. The guest bed had a new comforter and bed skirt, and the junior bed still wore its store tags.

Melba had obviously made a big effort to make everything warm and welcoming. Why did Sally have such different memories of her childhood? People don't change all that much. Sally was very glad she had come home to find her past.

Teddy stirred and rubbing her eyes with two tiny fists, said, "Mommy, are we there?"

Yes we are, sweet girl. We are at Grandma Melba's house. Taking Melba's hand in hers, Sally said, "This is your Grandma Melba." With that Teddy jumped up, opened her arms, gave Melba a hug, and exclaimed, "You're pretty, Grandma. You look just like my Mommy. I'm hungry Grandma. Can I have some milk?"

Melba smiled, "She doesn't need any warm up time, does she?" "No," Sally replied, "Teddy is definitely a people person." Melba went into the kitchen and brought a two-handled plastic kid's cup filled with milk and said, "This should keep you for a little while. They are expecting us for supper down at the restaurant."

"Are you still waitressing at the Four Corners, Mom?

"Well, you might say that, and I certainly do pitch in whenever I'm needed, but I bought the place 15 years ago, Sally. Last month we had a big party to celebrate the last mortgage payment. It's all mine, now. These days, I'm mostly at the cash register and in the bakery. How about we go on over and feed this hungry child?"

They piled into the rental. Sally turned right on Oak Street, which soon became Highway 92, and she drove about two miles to the Four Corners junction. The restaurant sat on the northeast corner, and Sally pulled in. Melba suggested they park in the back. The back entrance was a rustic wood door with a painted sign above it that read, "Melba's Blue Ribbon Bakery. State Fair First Prize Pies and Breads"

"What's this, Mom? I had no idea you'd opened a bakery." "Well, if I'd depended on my waitress wages and tips, it would have taken me forever to buy this place. The owners were getting up there in years and wanted to give me the chance to buy it, but I needed twenty-five thousand dollars to make it work and they didn't want to wait forever. I'd been entering the State Fair bake-offs every year and coming away with blue ribbons, so I asked if they would let me use the kitchen nights to do my breads and pies and put the money I earned toward my down payment. Before we knew what was happening every restaurant in town was giving us special orders, and then the folks over in Columbus City started ordering pies and coming over to pick them up and have dinner, too. I was working sixteen hours a day but I didn't mind because I was saving up fast. So there you have it! Now, let me show you the restaurant, and get Teddy a little something to tide her over."

The staff was obviously waiting for their arrival. When the three of them came through the kitchen doors, everybody clapped including Teddy and the customers. A corner table was nicely set for them with a white cloth and flowers and a big plate of choices for Teddy — chicken fingers, a peanut butter and jelly sandwich, and a bowl of macaroni and cheese. Around the bend covering one wall, there were newspaper clippings in simple black frames displaying articles by Sally or about Sally, and on the adjacent wall were blown-up photographs of Teddy, and a photograph of a handsome man that Sally correctly assumed was her father.

Sally was not prepared for this. She just took her mother into her arms, hugged her tight, kissed her on her cheek and then her forehead, and hand in hand, they walked to the table to sit with Teddy, to break bread together, and to open their hearts to one another. The day would soon come when they would share the painful episodes of their lives along with the good ones, expose the raw edges of their feelings with honesty, and at long last come to a place in the road where they could bury the hurt. Sally wanted to know more about her father, but that would have to wait for another day. On this day, her "cup runneth over."

Chapter 63

To plan their itinerary, Griff and his senior staff had gone over a comprehensive list of their accomplishments. They were amazed at the scope of the programs, and of the specific accomplishments of AID's short-term projects. Although Griff had been briefed on an ongoing basis, when it was laid out in detailed reports, even he was impressed by the wide array of completed projects.

The reports included the work of an Asian-African joint committee of GEI and AID, which was established to coordinate issues that related to drought. Effective methods to combat desert encroachment had been identified, and multiple programs and projects were underway.

On flood control, experts were working feverishly to develop more accurate flood-forecasting systems for the coastal areas of Asia and Africa most in danger. Underground dams and levees were under construction and considerable numbers of plants and trees had been strategically planted to reduce the threat.

In areas of critical food shortages, experiments related to sustainable agriculture had already made important inroads in alleviating hunger. For more productive farming in the rural areas, affordable electricity linking directly into the satellite solar system was in the initial stage of development, and technical centers in Asia and Africa were joined in a coordinating body to identify new rural electrification opportunities.

To ameliorate China's environmental problems, Jimmy Wu and experts from the University partnered with their Chinese counterparts to coordinate multi-tiered funding. With significant technical support from AID, new solid waste facilities in China were built with clean technologies that made for environmentally sound disposal; coal power plants, which were China's primary source of energy, were retrofitted with state-of-the-art clean coal technology, and the first-of-its-kind synthetic liquid gas facility in Beijing was nearly ready for operation. With target goals in China established by the Conference's China sub-committee on air pollution, staggered "no car" days were imposed by China's central government and enforced by the local governments in over 100 major cities. On those days, cars were banned from the main thoroughfares and on selected secondary roads as well. High-speed rail to connect urban centers was under construction and on its way to completion. The clean air progress would be slow but steady.

Jimmy was happy to give Chinese officials the lead in press conferences and technical papers, and he became a welcome consultant in their offices and a welcome guest in their homes. Chinese officials were beginning to be considered the world's authoritative voice for innovative clean air solutions, and they took great care to protect their budding leadership position.

In India, by 2024, a shortage of clean drinking water from both ground and surface water sources had created a severe water crisis. India's thriving economy and its rising population were causing huge demands on its fragile environment. More rainfall was falling in fewer days and Himalayan glaciers were in a melting cycle, bringing both droughts and floods. Sewage and wastewater from rapidly growing cities and industries had turned major rivers into putrid sewers. Extreme bouts of weather, a deteriorating water distribution infrastructure and a lack of water allocation rules added to challenges that could not be addressed without government action.

This was a scenario that was perfect for Raj Singh and the Sub-Continent committee of GEI. Managed by Singh and a co-chair from New Delhi, the water distribution infastructure was repaired where it could be, and a massive construction project was underway to rebuild it where repairs could not do the job. Water allocation rules were politically complicated to achieve but a sincere and concerted effort was underway and beginning to demonstrate results.

These projects would take years to complete so Raj was spending a lot of his time now with his parents who had returned to Mumbai and was accepted by Indian officials as one of their own. He and his New Delhi co-chair would become avid spokesmen world wide for clean water initiatives and sought-after speakers on drought and flooding. This became Raj's second career and his life's work.

As for Saudi Arabia and Iran, Amos and Griff could not be more pleased. The perpetrators of misery had morphed into the valuable crown jewels. From King Khalid and President Zahedi's failed attempt to disrupt America's energy supply and the kidnapping that followed in its wake, to a successful AID endeavor to diversify the Saudi and Iranian economies, it was clear that change was coming. It was plain that the old ways were giving way to new ones, that the narrow thinking of old men was shifting to the fresher thinking of younger ones, that the old world of greed and absolute power was tranforming into a new world of good governance and economic opportunity for ordinary people.

Griff came home with an itinerary that he knew would please Amos, and he was satisfied that solid groundwork for the big tour had been laid. With an abundance of details to deal with, Griff returned to his desk and rolled up his sleeves.

Chapter 64

After Winn's funeral, Mitch Norman went to work for Senator James Mason Clark, Winn's successor. Just as Winn had taken him on without a background check, so had Clark. After Mitch's teen years as a Senate page and the internships he held during his college years, he floated around the Hill working in one job or another and became a familiar face to anyone who had been around for a while. He was respected for his technical expertise in automating just about everything and for getting the machinery of a busy office operating in a well-oiled and efficient way. As far as computers were concerned, Mitch could program or fix anything, and when other Senate offices had a particularly difficult computer problem that their techs couldn't handle, they would call him in to see if he could.

Mitch, who got his Masters degree in Political Science at American University, was also familiar with the institutional workings of the House and the Senate. He knew how to bird-dog a piece of legislation and he was skillful at working with other administrative assistants on complicated bills to make sure their bosses understood what it was they were voting for or against. He was indispensable to a busy Senator who spent most of his days in Committee meetings, hearings, giving speeches, meeting with bundlers, schmoosing at fundraising gatherings, or campaigning back in his home state.

He was also indispensable to his father, Spencer al Nouri, a second-generation American of Syrian descent. Al Nouri headed an organization whose richly funded and well-concealed purpose was to rid the Arab world of American influence and to overthrow the State of Israel. His family had lost its farmland near Lake Tiberius in the Golan Heights during the '67 war with Israel, but he insisted that it belonged to them, it was still in their name, and he wanted it back. In spite of his highly successful life in America and without regard to facts on the ground in a thriving Syria satisfied with the peace treaty they had negotiated with Israel, he was still filled with deep hatred for the Israelis and for their American allies. It was a nearly 60-year-old hatred passed on through the generations by stories that bore little resemblance to reality; tales that were embellished until they possessed only fragments of the truth.

Al Nouri's fund, the Alliance for Mid-East Peace and Prosperity, was located in the sub-basement of his home in northern Virginia. In the late '80s, when the Syrian-Iranian alliance was forged to control Lebanon, al Nouri was the recipient of significant start-up funding from both nations. His job as Executive Director was to raise money in America ostensibly to support what appeared to be worthwhile social service projects for struggling Arab refugees. Some of the funds were necessarily channeled into good works, but most of the money was used to support the training and arming of terrorist militias, especially Hezbollah. Mitch knew almost nothing of his father's covert activities and believed that since he was the oldest son, he was chosen to learn the legitimate business of the Alliance.

Spencer al Nouri was a computer wizard. There were a dozen or so computers in al Nouri's subterranean office and Spencer taught Mitch everything a computer geek should know, and some things he shouldn't know such as the ins and outs of cyber-hacking. From the time he was allowed in that room, eleven-year-old Mitch understood that it was a secret place that only he and his father could access. When they entered it, his father locked the door behind them, and when they left, his father locked the door and punched in numbers on the keypad. His exhausted mother was busy taking care of his five younger siblings, and had no inclination to question her son's or her husband's long absences in a sub-basement that was off limits to her. She assumed Mitch was doing his homework, and that Spencer was doing his work, and since she had everything she wanted, she was content.

Only when Mitch was safely rooted in his Senate staff trajectory did he learn of his father's expectations, and by then the father-son bond was too strong to break. After serving for several years as the legislative aide for Winn's friend, a Senator from Virginia who was chairman of the Committee on Foreign Relations, Mitch went to work as the administrative assistant in Winn's Senate office. The Virginia Senator was retiring and Mitch came highly recommended.

Al Nouri was both the chief cyber-hacker and the central banker of the energy supply code-breaking scheme and was told to direct his son Mitch to track Griff from the first moment of Winn's assassination. But Griff had played it smart and a terrified Mitch, surrounded with other staffers and law enforcement officials from the early hours of the occurrence, was trapped. Then Griff disappeared and everything spun out of control.

The Study Commissions appointed by the President to review the incident were about to issue their reports. A nervous Mitch knew from his cyber-hacking that in addition to pointing out the weaknesses that had enabled the culprits to perform their misdeeds, they were also going to point a finger at someone in Winn's inner circle, someone who knew that Winn was about to reveal the plot, someone who had the tech savvy to hack into Winn's secured computer network. It was getting too close for comfort.

Mitch text messaged his father, and they set a time and place to meet for dinner.

Chapter 65

Molly Bentsen was in her office reading DIA's draft report for the second time. It had been hand-delivered to her red-stamped CONFIDENTIAL — FOR EYES ONLY. The report was titled STUDY OF FAILED EFFORT TO BREAK TOP SECRET ENERGY SECURITY CODES" and sub-titled, "The Vulnerabilities of U.S. Energy Cyberspace Networks and the Critical Changes Needed to Secure Them." Attached was a flow-chart describing the trail that led to dozens of computers, some at an unknown location, some in the Saudi and Iranian embassies, some in Riyadh and Tehran, some in off-shore banks, two at NASA, three at the State Department, two at the U.S. Mission House at the UN, one in the UN Secretary General's office, one in the Eisenhower Building's NSA office, one in her own NSA safe-room, and two still active in Winn's old Senate office. Dates were attached to the communications, with a list of addressees. Molly already knew about the trail of electronic records that had done in the culprits who had pled out their crimes, but this was both a treasure trove and a time bomb. There was a yellow post-it bottom right that said "Molly, Call me! TM." She called the Admiral on his private line.

Retired Rear Admiral Thomas Mallory, Director of the Pentagon's Defense Intelligence Agency picked up the phone. "Molly, we need to go deep on this. I'll give you ten minutes and I'll call you back." Molly understood she needed to take the Admiral's call from the Situation Room, which was free of listening devices and was swept several times a day just to make sure it was clean. She hustled down to the basement room to take the call.

The DIA's wide-ranging expertise in the computer sciences was hailed throughout the U.S. Intelligence community and even beyond.

Defense policemakers and force planners turned to these computer wizards for anything crucial, and Molly supposed Amos knew exactly what he was doing when he assigned this job to the Admiral's shop. Molly took the call and the Admiral said, "Molly, I'm thinking that the DIA report is too damn hot to turn in officially but it is also too anticipated to bury. We have got a ton of intel backup from our intercepts and even more from our white hat hackers. I don't think we can release the report and let it fall into congressional hands. Even if we confine it to the leaders and the intel committees, you know as well as I do, that it'll leak. I took it upon myself to block the Independent Commission from getting anywhere close to this stuff. Now that their report is coming out, I hear from our sources they have got a ton of complaints in it about denial of access, and we need to figure out how to handle their complaints and what to do with my report. Let's meet and make some decisions. I'm already cleared for the Situation Room, and I can be there in twenty minutes if that suits you. I'll depend on you to notify the front gate. Okay?"

Molly was fond of the Admiral but she was definitely not looking forward to the meeting. She had an uneasy feeling in the pit of her stomach that there was trouble ahead. Amos had let her off the hook on the poorly vetted NSC people she had hired, and she promised herself she would do everything in her considerable power to shield him.

Admiral Mallory arrived and laid out the loose pages of the flow charts on the conference table. "Molly, we have got a Pandora's Box here. If we disclose the details, we revive our differences with the Iranians and the Saudis. We have got that situation pretty much under control now, and it is just the wrong time to light a fire that's been put out."

"The new Iranian leadership is beginning to secure a foothold, and we don't want to do anything that will put them on the defensive or give meat to the radicals who have scurried underground for now. As far as the Saudis are concerned, King Khalid is on a new path, a hopeful path, and I say 'let sleeping dogs lie'. As far as the rest of the report is concerned, we've already implemented the security recommendations; some of it is old news, but some of it is very troubling and needs to be dealt with."

"Our white hats have uncovered ongoing high-security-coded messaging from Winn's old Senate office to computers we haven't been able to locate. That's never happened to us before and I have to admit that we are frustrated. The daily messaging went on from Winn's first day on the job and has continued from Senator's Clark's office without interruption. We have got to know what that's all about, and we have got to do it expeditiously and below the radar. The last thing we want to do is sully Winn's name, or drag Griff into this if there's no reason to. We can't get away with Amos' tactics on the security breach arrests a second time. That was an emergency situation. On this, we have to be careful to do it legally, and we'll need Justice to guide us on that.

"As I see it, we need a FISA Court Order that will enable us to confiscate the computers as soon as we find them, along with an unambiguous directive to keep a lid on the information we unearth. But, we also can't have anyone slip out from under. What's your read on this, Molly?"

"Admiral, I think we are on the same wavelength." Molly replied. "On the Commission reports, my gut reaction is to classify them Top Secret and archive them for fifty years. Use Executive Powers if Justice tells us we need them! The President can use his considerable communication skills to call the members personally, assure them that he will seriously consider their recommendations and ease them into the plan. I can work directly with the Commission's Counsel to draft an Abstract that can be released"

"After the release of the Abstract, the President can bring the members into the Oval office, give them each an impressive plaque and a photo, and then have them up to the residence for dinner to sooth any damaged egos."

"On the intercepts, it sounds serious, but you are the expert and I have complete confidence that you will deal with that situation in the best possible way. It would be a big help if we had the hackers in hand to go along with the Abstract."

"Thanks for the vote of confidence. We'll do our best. We're working hard on a lead. In the course of our investigation, we checked out every staffer"s personnel records in Winn's offices and in the offices of his successor. No background check was found in Mitch Norman's file. For starters, we already know that Mitch Norman is not his legal name, but there could be a legitimate explanation for that. We've got Personnel working on it, but with a light hand. If he's involved, we don't want to scare him off. Just in case, though, we've put a tail on him."

"How do you want to handle bringing Amos up to date?"

"If its okay with you, Admiral, I'd like to brief the President alone, give him some breathing room in case he needs it. If he has anything to add to our conversation, I'll let you know."

"Fine with me, Molly. Amos is a good man. You keep looking out for him."

Chapter 66

Spencer al Nouri and his son, Mitch Norman met for dinner in Alexandria, Virginia at the Cedar Knoll Inn, a Mediterranean restaurant overlooking the Potomac River. It was a chilly day, but they chose to sit at a table on the deck.

"Pa, I think I'm in trouble, and if I am, you are too. Somebody has been sniffing around in my personnel files and hacking into my office computers. Personnel asked me to fill out what they call "a missing paper to complete my file', which includes a space for my addresses dating back to my first job on the Hill, and one for the names of my parents, strictly a "file requirement'. Obviously, they are on to something and I have to surmise it's nothing that's good for me. You have to destroy your hard drives and the backup discs pretty fast. I am selectively doing that with mine, but my job is harder. I can't destroy all the Senate files, so I have to dig around for the files I need to purge. As soon as the job is done, I'm quitting and taking off. Please destroy your stuff now, Pa. Otherwise we could both end up with very tight nooses around our very guilty necks. Maybe we should pack up the family and hide out with our relatives in Detroit until we see how the wind is blowing. Or take a trip to Syria or Lebanon if we can get out of the country. This is probably the end of the road for the Alliance. It's been on shaky ground for a while, anyway."

"Don't panic, Mitch. I have cyber-tricks even you don't know about. If they locate my computers, they will end up in the Internet Café on Pier 3 of the Reagan Airport. I agree you should take off for a while. I'll arrange for you to stay with Ma's sister. I'm going to sit tight. I'll be on the lookout for hackers, but I can easily throw them off course.

You forget, Mitch, I'm the best in the business. Now, let's have a good meal."

What Spencer didn't know was that there had been a tail on Mitch for the past week. Two FBI men were seated inside the restaurant with a full view of the patio, and an FBI man and woman were strolling hand in hand along the riverbank. Spencer was going to lead the inside team right to his doorstep. The couple appearing to take a leisurely walk along the riverbank would continue to follow Mitch.

At about 9 o'clock, Spencer gave Mitch a big bear hug, took his face into both of his hands, heartily kissed him on both cheeks and patted him on the back. Then father and son parted. A second car joined the team that was following Spencer. When they called in they were told the FISA paperwork was done; they had subpoenas and a green light to raid the premises, arrest al Nouri and confiscate the computers. Spencer pulled into his garage. They gave him ten minutes. Three more cars pulled up with the paperwork, the building was surrounded, and two men knocked at the front door.

An unsuspecting Mrs. al Nouri opened the door wearing an apron and wiping her hands on a kitchen towel. The men flashed their badges and asked to see her husband. She said he was in his office in the sub basement and pointed to the staircase. They told her to gather her family and wait in the kitchen. Two uniformed women stepped up to accompany them into the kitchen

Then all hell broke loose. The door to the sub-basement office was locked and it took the brute force of some very big guys to knock it down. Spencer was caught frantically trying to cleanse his computers. The agents handed him the subpoenas and Spencer, a smart man who understood that the game was over, voluntarily put his hands behind his back and turned around to make it easy for the agents to handcuff him. On his way out the front door, he turned to his bewildered wife and simply shrugged his shoulders.

At midnight, four computer geeks from DIA arrived accompanied by armed military guards and began working at the computers. Several hours later, the computers were transported to the DIA Analysis Center at Bolling Air Force base in D.C.

Mitch was arrested as he was parking his car and offered no resistance. He figured he had waited too long to get out from under his father's thumb, and he deserved to be caught. He was relieved that it was over.

Justice is not a perfect science. Spencer's obsessive appetite for his ancestral farmland, which had long ago disappeared into the warp and weave of a new Syria, had driven him into a ruinous struggle with his reason. For him, justice was one thing; for others, it was something else.

Chapter 67

Griff and Amos set off on the big tour with Raj Singh, Jimmy Wu and an entourage of Secret Service agents, cabinet secretaries, staff and press. At each stop, from the coastal towns and forests of South America and Africa to the big cities of China and India to the coastal regions of Southeast Asia and finally to the Middle East nations of Iran and Saudi Arabia, Amos was hailed as a larger than life hero and greeted by leaders and dignitaries as a true friend of the earth, a good steward of the land and its people.

The advance teams that Griff had pulled together had done a masterful job of providing suitable speech venues, colorful native dinners and events, meetings with the appropriate leaders, but most importantly, they made sure that Amos saw the upshot of his dreams. He saw children thriving in villages where there had been starvation. He saw new dams and clean rivers where there had been only filth. He saw fledgling forests and fertile farms where there had been baren land and desert. He saw new towns and paved roads in places where there had been only dirt roads and hovels. He drank clean water and he breathed clean air. He saw his imaginings emerge before his eyes as real as the steady beating of his heart. He had accomplished as much as any man could in merely eight years, and he was satisfied.

Amos and Griff especially enjoyed their stop in Jeddah. The King was aging and ailing and he had mellowed. He welcomed them in a special ceremony reserved for friends of the Kingdom and expressed his profound gratitude. After the ceremony, Crown Prince Nayif joined them on a trek down the new roads, past the canals and dams to the farms and towns that now dotted the desert sands.

Nayif introduced them to the Saudi workers and to the many foreign workers who toiled alongside them, workers who had eagerly journeyed from other lands and cultures to lend their skills to build a dream. He took them on a tour of the greenhouses and processing plants and escorted them to his home for the evening meal. There they met Aiaisha and the three little ones, an infant, a pretty girl just beginning to toddle, and a handsome boy three years of age. Amos heart melted as it always did in the presence of little ones. He got on his knees to speak eye to eye with the boy, and in the boy's eyes he saw the promise of a tomorrow of friendship and understanding between people with very different traditions. He knew it was possible because he had just seen a glimpse of it.

Amos was not much of a church-going man, but he was a believer and this visit with Nayif and his young family tapped the deep spiritual dimension in him that always rested just beneath the surface. When the desert winds whistled through the tall palms in Nayif's walled garden, he thought he heard a voice whispering, "Well done, Amos, well done." He had been gifted with enormous power and he had put it to good use. He knew he would miss it. What mountains could he climb from here?

An intuitive man, Griff reflected that it was going to be difficult for Amos to transition to a normal life from a world inconceivable to those who had never experienced it. He, too, was feeling pangs of regret that this amazing journey was coming to an end. Griff was thankful that Sally and Teddy were waiting for him back home. That made all the difference.

Years passed and Nayif continued in a high profile role at each annual conference. Kathy Asher was now working as a Deputy Secretary of State. She could no longer contain her need to see him again and arranged to attend a conference seminar that Nayif was leading. Kathy approached him at the end of the session. The years had been kind to her and he recognized her at once.

Cautiously weighing her words, Kathy said, "Prince Nayif, I just want to congratulate you on your extraordinary accomplishments. You are high on the State Department's list of our friends in the Middle East. I am now a Deputy Secretary, and if there is ever anything I can ever do to help you, please don't hesitate to call me." Kathy handed Nayif her card.

In this new age Nayif no longer felt constrained by the old Muslim boundaries, and he took both of Kathy's hands into both of his, and with great tenderness in his voice, he said, "You have already helped me in so many important ways, Kathy. I have never forgotten any of them. I have never forgotten those astonishing days of my youthful awakening. You taught me things beyond my imaginings, and my life was changed forever. I am a happy man because you taught me how to open my feelings to the feelings of others. You taught me that there is no shame in intimacy, and armed with that knowledge, my wife, Aiaisha, and I are everything that we could ever hope to be. Until the end of my sojourn on this earth, you would be an honored guest in the Kingdom."

"Thank you, Nayif. Knowing that the memory of us is still with you as vividly as it is with me somehow releases me to move forward. Since you, I have found a thousand reasons for turning away new chances for happiness. Now, perhaps I can be whole again. I'm going to give it a try."

With a gentle grasp of hands, they parted, each to his and her own life, each to his and her own memories, and each many miles from the misguided pathways of their earlier days.

Nayif returned home after this 12th Annual Conference, and was immediately summoned to King Khalid's Palace in Jeddah. The King sat very still in his large chair in the Inner Courtyard and waited for the Crown Prince to approach him. He motioned for Nayif to place his ear at his mouth. "I have been very ill, Nayif, and my strength is ebbing," whispered the King, "Do not fret, my dear nephew, for my soul is eager to fly away to the Gates of Paradise. I was sometimes foolish in my ways, and I pray that the Scales of Justice will be kind and allow me to enter. You are of a more enlightened time and you will be a wiser ruler than I knew how to be. Remember always that you hold the interests of our people in your hands. With the help of Allah, you will be a great King. Peace be upon you."

"Allah hu Akbar."

"Allah hu Akbar."

With that, the King dropped his head, a bit of spittle dripped from the corners of his mouth, a guttural sound escaped his throat, and he was dead.

A big green bird perched on the head frame of the King's chair and fluttered its wings but did not fly away until the King was lifted from his chair and carried toward the Palace. Then the green bird took off in frenzied flight, circled the Palace until its doors were fastened, and flew straight up to touch a brilliant sky.

In Islam, there is a belief that a big green bird comes to take the soul of the dead into its heart to fly it to the Gates of Paradise. Nayif believed he saw this come to pass before his very eyes. He sat motionless in the Courtyard until night fell. Then he entered his new dwelling.

Chapter 68

Amir was tired of hiding. He learned from the newspaper, which he scrounged daily from one trash bin or another that the King was dead, and maybe, just maybe he could finally return home. Long ago, he read that Li had been deported, and he knew the laptop and the tapes no longer existed because he had destroyed them. The only thing those records could ever have accomplished was to get him and a lot of other people in big trouble.

On the night of the rescue, Amir tucked away the limo in the empty old barn of some adjacent backland farm property whose absent owners were simply waiting to cash out when the new road came through. He had caught a shadow of Li talking on her cell that night, and he didn't want to take any chances. He grabbed the laptop, gathered the tapes and threw them into a garbage bag, hurriedly packed some food and took off in the limo across a rear dirt road. The road ended in a briar patch, but Amir had scouted out an escape route earlier and was familiar with a tractor trail that led up to an abandoned barn. Once there, he smashed the laptop with the remnants of some farm tools that were scattered around and buried its bits and pieces, carefully burned the tapes in a controlled way and camped out in the barn for almost a week.

Leaving the limo behind and well hidden, he took off on foot for a well-known enclave in Rock Creek Park that harbored drifters. It didn't take long for Amir to find the eerie heavily wooded place in the Park that was to become his hobo home. His newfound acquaintances named him The Arab and gave him a spot on the muddy soil where he could lay his head down on some newspaper and cardboard and later on the smelly sleeping bag of a dead man. Some faces came and left. Some faces came and stayed and some befriended him and told him their names and their stories. Some were winos, some unbalanced, some just desperate men like himself seeking refuge for one reason or another. There were no women in this place. It was too rugged, too wild for them here. Once in a while the Park Police came by and told the group to move along, and they would go through the motions, but the Police would move on and they would move back. To this motley collection of vagrants, the shade of the trees gave them some protection in the sunlight of summer, and in winter the canopy of branches became a roof to catch the falling snow.

It wasn't long before the expensive clothing on Amir's back was dirty and frayed, and the money he had brought with him was nearly gone. He used the park restroom to clean himself up, got some decent used clothes at the homeless shelter where he sometimes grabbed a hot meal, took jobs as a day laborer, a dishwasher, an ice cream cart driver, and even occasionally resorted to panhandling. Froggy, a gnarled old man with a huge lump protruding from the middle of his forehead, was Amir's daily companion, the one he trusted to watch his things while he worked his occasional jobs.

Living in the woods, the once smooth skin of Amir's face began to wrinkle with wind burned cheeks; grime now blackened the lines, and his nasty jobs tore at his once manicured fingernails. He no longer felt the paralyzing fear that had gripped him and sent him on the run, but being homeless had become a full time job. Now he was trapped, consumed by the moment, with just getting up in the morning and getting through the long day. If he ever escaped this pitiless place, he would go home and live an observant and respectable life.

Amir worked up the courage to call his old contact at the Saudi Embassy, which was not too far from his Park hideaway, and he told him he wanted to come in. He said that he hoped he would be treated as Li had been and deported to his homeland. The contact was friendly because he figured that despite the stretch of time gone by, Amir might still be radioactive. He could be dealt with better politically, one way or the other, if he was in Saudi custody, and he was encouraged to come to the Embassy.

Collecting his few possessions, Amir said his goodbyes, especially to Froggy, and he took off. He figured he would cross Rock Creek Parkway and make his way down to New Hampshire to the Embassy. When there was a lull in the fast traffic, Amir started across the Parkway. He heard a voice shouting at him, turned around and saw Froggy waving the flashlight Amir had unintentionally left behind. Just then a speeding car came toward Froggy and tried to brake; Amir ran, pushed Froggy out of harm's way and was hit by the front fender of the car and crushed to death beneath its wheels. Froggy bent over his only friend's broken body and wept.

A big green bird circled around Amir and sat on the car roof until a police ambulance carted him off. The green bird followed the ambulance along the Parkway and across Massachusetts Avenue to the City morgue, flying around until the ambulance disappeared beneath the building. If Amir's final act had tipped the Scales in his favor, he was going home.

Chapter 69

Thanksgiving came only two months before the end of Amos last term as President, and Betsy wanted to spend it at the White House with her special family. So it was that on the Thanksgiving Day of 2032, this family gathered around the dining table in the White House Residence, Betsy and Amos, Celeste and Charles, Feld, Sarah and Melanie, Arthur and Pamela, Sally, Griff and Teddy, and a new addition to the list, Melba Burton.

Ever since Sally's reunion with her mother, they spoke at least once a week, and little by little they learned the details of their separate lives. Sally finally learned about her father, Randy Burton. Melba explained that she met Randy when he was passing through town with the State Fair. He called the square dances, ran the games, and was handy enough to keep the rusting rides going. As Melba told it, he was tall and lean with a fine-chiselled face and gaunt high cheekbones that wrapped around his deepset eyes. But it was his smile that captivated her most of all. It was a smile that lit up the room.

Randy fell just as hard for Sally as she fell for him. Her youth and innocence touched a chord in his world-weary soul. Twenty-eight years earlier, only a few hours after his birth, he was abandoned at a firehouse station entrance and abusive alcoholic parents adopted him. At four years of age, he became a ward of the State and was raised in one foster home after another.

Randy's story, which most of us like to think happens only in a Dickens tale, actually took place in the hardscrabble slums of Cincinnatti, a place where poverty and desperation were daily companions. There, life as a foster kid stuck on the wrong side of the tracks was as hard as it gets. Shuffled from pillar to post, Randy never had a chance to form any lasting relationships. At seventeen, he hit the highway, thumbed a ride, and he had been on the road ever since. Carnivals and State Fairs became his destination. He felt at home with carny people. They never questioned. They never judged. They shared whatever they had, whether it was a beer from a beer vendor, hot dogs or a burger from a restaurant stand, or conversation and a spare bed. He could always hitch a ride to the next stop or the next town, depending upon whether he was in a dark mood or a happy one. His moods were something he didn't understand but when they came, they crushed him with a restlessness he just couldn't shake. During those bad times, he hopped a train and rode the rails until the mood passed.

The amazing thing was that Randy stayed with Melba for as long as he did. He adored her and he adored Sally. He settled in, worked at the processing plant, picked up extra money at harvest time, and got home to tend Sally so Melba could go off to her waitress job at Four Corners. When the State Fair came to town, Randy's bosses willingly gave him the green light to to take three weeks off to work there.

To an outsider, Melba and Randy Burton appeared to be a typical small town family, scratching out a modest living but making it just fine. Except, Melba knew all was not well. Sometimes Randy went for days without speaking, and once in a while he spent all night sitting on the porch rocking hard. There were times when they made love and Randy would take her face between his big hands and just stare at her. In those moments, Melba saw a profound sadness etched in his face that was unsettling. It was this stare that was the last thing Melba remembered. Randy left a note on the dresser saying he was going fishing with his buddies, packed extra jeans and shoes, took his only jacket, and he was gone. When Melba read the note she knew he wasn't coming back. A deeply religious Melba believed that this was God's will;

just as she accepted that it was all right for Sally to build a life away from home that didn't include her.

There was no bitterness in Melba. She never stopped loving Randy or Sally. The things that were beyond her control she mentally placed in a jar and put up on a shelf. But she was determined to use every ounce of her God-given talents to make something of herself. She had dreamed of owning the restaurant and she owned it. She was delighted by the surprise of a successful bakery and she was making the most of it. But she never dreamed that she would be in this high place surrounded by all these wonderful people who had made room for her in their hearts. She never imagined that one day her daughter and granddaughter would be sitting by her side. On this Thanksgiving Day, she said a silent prayer of thanks to the God she believed had planned it all.

Amos lifted his glass and in a voice that was both tender and strong, he bowed his head and prayed, "Those of us who sit at this Thanksgiving table are blessed beyond measure. We are blessed to live in this free nation where opportunity knows no boundaries, where we are granted freedom to worship as we choose, freedom to differ and to speak of our differences, and freedom to walk our own path. We have been blessed by the extraordinary friendship and love that binds us together, and we have been doubly blessed by the presence of our beloved Teddy who provides the glue. Each year, may we come together on this day of Thanksgiving to give thanks to God, the Author of all of these blessings and to renew our pledge to Him that we will gladly share our bounty with those who have less. Let us, each in our own way, thank Him for the food we are about to receive. Amen."

Betsy said she wanted to say a few words too. "Today, I look at the faces at this table and I am happy and whole and thankful. Next Thanksgiving we will be in our new home in North Carolina, a big barn of a place that has room enough for all of you. I will keep reminding you that we very much want you to come. Sarah has promised to bring Feld and Melanie along with her apple strudel and thumbprint cookies; Melba will bake her yummy pies in my new kitchen; Amos will do his famous deep fried turkey and I'll back it up for the Felds and the weight watchers with a kosher one roasted on the spit of our kitchen barbeque. Of course, we will depend on Celeste and Charles to do their lovely flower arrangements, and on all of us to do the feasting, and Teddy, just as I promised, there will a Shetland pony for you to ride. Since you are helping Amos with the Library, Griff, I know we will be seeing you during the year, but we are counting on you and Sally for Thanksgiving, and on you, Arthur and Pamela to complete our wonderful family."

"I hope I have put all of you on the spot sufficiently to guarantee that, God willing, next year's Thanksgiving table will look just like this one. Now, let's get on with the feasting."

On such a happy day, it was best relegated to ancient history that the lives of these good people had once been touched by the evil conspiracies of greedy men. If there is a spark of the divine concealed in even the most evil acts, that spark created this unique family, born of happenstance, bound by struggle, and sealed by love. Changes will come as they always do, but the spirit of this family is changeless for it is woven into the thread that goes on forever.

When this thread emerged from the mist that curled around the giant oak tree near where he lay, Winston Ainsley understood the hidden purpose of his leaving, and he was content at last.

Printed in the United States
153556LV00002B/27/P

9 781449 003791